Twin

When Dr. R...
kidney transp...
steps in to help—changing their lives forever!
As these twin docs start over, it might be time
for them to meet their perfect match!

Second Chance with Her Guarded GP

Starting work in a new practice, GP Ollie Langley
hadn't anticipated falling for gorgeous
nurse practitioner Gemma Baxter! Dare he
take a risk on love?

Baby Miracle for the ER Doc

When Dr. Rob Langley meets ER doc
Florence Jacobs, sparks fly! And one special night
leads to life-changing consequences.

Both titles available now!

NORFOLK ITEM

30129 080 865 133

Dear Reader,

What would you do for someone you love?

When Ollie's twin, Rob, needs a kidney, Ollie immediately offers to be a living donor—but his fiancée can't cope and calls off their wedding. Ollie's hurt and guarded and doesn't plan to get involved again...until he meets Gemma.

Gemma's overcome the worst: losing her little sister to a virus that affected her heart. She does adventurous things to raise money for medical research so other families won't lose someone they love. She doesn't want a relationship, either...until she meets Ollie.

Ollie and Gemma are drawn to each other despite their differences. Can they help heal each other's past hurts and move forward to the future they both want but are too scared to reach for?

I hope you enjoy Ollie and Gemma's journey (and the seals)!

With love,

Kate Hardy

SECOND CHANCE
WITH HER GUARDED GP

KATE HARDY

HARLEQUIN

MEDICAL
ROMANCE

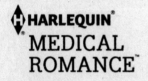

HARLEQUIN®
MEDICAL
ROMANCE™

Recycling programs
for this product may
not exist in your area.

ISBN-13: 978-1-335-40877-8

Second Chance with Her Guarded GP

Harlequin Enterprises ULC
22 Adelaide St. West, 40th Floor
Toronto, Ontario M5H 4E3, Canada
www.Harlequin.com

Printed in U.S.A.

Kate Hardy has always loved books and could read before she went to school. She discovered Harlequin novels when she was twelve and decided that this was what she wanted to do. When she isn't writing, Kate enjoys reading, cinema, ballroom dancing and the gym. You can contact her via her website, katehardy.com.

Books by Kate Hardy

Harlequin Medical Romance

Visit the Author Profile page
at Harlequin.com for more titles.

For Vicki Ward Hibbins,
with love and thanks for the seal light bulb!

CHAPTER ONE

OLIVER LANGLEY TOOK a deep breath.

This was it. His new start. Not the life he'd thought he'd have, six months ago: but that had been before the world had tilted on its axis and mixed everything up. Before his twin brother Rob had gone to work for a humanitarian aid organisation in the aftermath of an earthquake and his appendix had burst. Before Rob had ended up with severe blood poisoning that had wiped out his kidneys. Before Ollie had donated a kidney to his twin.

Before Ollie's fiancée had called off their wedding.

Which had been his own fault for asking her to move the wedding. 'Tab, with Rob being on dialysis, he's not well enough even to be at the wedding, let alone be my best man.' He'd been so sure his fiancée would see things the same way that he did. It made perfect sense to move the wedding until after the transplant, giving both him and Rob time to recover from the operation and meaning that Ollie's entire family would be there to share the day. 'Let's move the wedding back a few months. The transplant's hopefully going to be at the beginning of June, so we'll both be properly recovered by August. We can have a late summer wedding instead.'

'Move the wedding.' It had been a statement, not a question. She'd gone silent, as if considering it, then shaken her head. 'No.'

He'd stared at her. 'Tab, I know it'll be a bit of work, changing all the arrangements, but I'll do as much of it as I can.'

'That's not what I mean, Ollie.'

He'd stared at her, not understanding. 'Then what do you mean?'

'I—I've been thinking for a while. We should call it off.'

'Call it off?' He'd gone cold. 'Why? Have you met someone else?'

'No. It's not you. It's me.'

Which meant the problem *was* him and she was trying to be nice. 'Tab, whatever it is, we can work it out. Whatever I've done to upset you, I'm sorry.' He loved her. He wanted to marry her, to make a family with her. He'd thought she felt the same way and wanted the same things. But it was becoming horribly clear that he'd got it all wrong.

Her eyes had filled with tears. 'It's not you, it's me,' she said again. 'You're giving Rob a kidney—of course you are. He's your brother and you love him. Anyone would do the same, in your shoes.'

'But?' He'd forced himself to say the word she'd left out.

She'd looked him in the eye. 'What if something goes wrong? What if *you* get ill, and your one remaining kidney doesn't work any more, and you have to go on dialysis? What if they can't find a match for you, and you die?'

'That's not going to happen, Tab.' He'd tried to put his arms round her to comfort and reassure her but she'd pulled away.

'You're not listening, Ollie. I can't do this.'

'Why?'

'You know how it's been with my dad.'

'Yes.' Tabby's father had chronic fatigue syndrome. He'd been too ill to do much for years.

'Mum stuck by her wedding vows—in sickness and in health. I didn't realise when I was younger, but she worked herself to the bone, making sure my brother and I were OK, and keeping us financially afloat, and looking after Dad. Obviously when we got older and realised how ill Dad was, Tom and I did as much as we could do to help. But my mum's struggled every single day, Ollie. She's sacrificed her life to look after Dad. And I can't do that for you. I just *can't.*'

He'd frowned. 'But I'm not ill, Tab. OK, I'll need a bit of time to recover from the transplant, but I'll be fine. Rob will get better and everything will be back to normal soon enough.'

'But you can't promise me you'll always be well and I won't have to look after you, Ollie. You can't possibly promise something like that.' Tabby had shaken her head. 'I'm sorry, Ollie. I can't marry you.' She'd fought to hold back the tears. 'I know it's selfish and I know it's unfair, but I just don't love you enough to take that risk. I don't want a life like my mum's. I don't want to marry you.' She'd taken off the engagement ring and given it back to him. 'I'm so sorry, Ollie. But I can't do this.'

'Tab, you've just got an attack of cold feet. We'll get through this,' he said. 'We love each other. It'll be fine.'

'No, Ollie. That's the point. I do love you— but not *enough.* I'm sorry.'

He hadn't been able to change her mind.

She'd got in touch to wish him and Rob

luck with the transplant, but she'd made it clear she didn't want him back. He wasn't enough for her. To the point where she hadn't even wanted him to help cancel all the arrangements; Tabby insisted on doing it all herself.

Ollie had spent a couple of weeks brooding after the operation, and he'd realised that he needed some time away from London. So he'd taken a six-month sabbatical from the practice in Camden where he was a salaried GP, lent his flat to a friend, and had gone back to Northumbria to stay with Rob and their parents. The open skies, hills and greenery had given him a breathing space from the bustle of London and time to think about what he wanted to do with his life.

Though the enforced time off after the transplant, once he'd untangled the wedding, had left Ollie with the fidgets. Much as he loved their parents and completely understood why their mum was fussing over her twin boys, Ollie liked having his own space and the smothering was driving him mad. He was pretty sure that doing the job he loved would help him get his equilibrium back and help him move on from the mess of his wedding-that-wasn't.

Then he'd seen the ad for a three-month

maternity cover post at Ashermouth Bay Surgery, which would take him nearly up to the end of his sabbatical. He'd applied for the job; once the practice had given him a formal offer, he'd found a three-month let and moved into one of the old fishermen's cottages near the harbour, within walking distance of the practice.

And today was his first day at his new job. He might not have been enough for his fiancée, but he knew he was definitely good enough as a doctor.

The building was single-storey, built of red brick and with a tiled roof. There were window-boxes filled with welcoming bright red geraniums, and a raised brick flower bed in front of the door, filled with lavender. The whole place looked bright and welcoming; and next to the door was a sign listing the practice staff, from the doctors and nurses through to the reception and admin team.

Ollie was slightly surprised to see his own name on the sign, underneath that of Aadya Devi, the GP whose maternity leave he was covering, but it made him feel welcome. Part of the team. He really liked that.

He took a deep breath, pushed the door open and walked in to the reception area.

The receptionist was chatting to a woman

in a nurse's uniform, who had her back to him. Clearly neither of them had heard him come in, because they were too busy talking about him.

'Dr Langley's starting this morning,' the receptionist said.

'Our newbie,' the nurse said, sounding pleased.

At thirty, Ollie didn't quite see himself as a 'newbie', but never mind. He was new to the practice, so he supposed it was an accurate description.

'Caroline's asked me to help him settle in, as she's away this week,' the nurse added.

Caroline was the senior partner at the practice: a GP in her late fifties, with a no-nonsense attitude and a ready laugh. Ollie had liked her very much at the interview.

He didn't really need someone to help him settle in, but OK. He got that this place was a welcoming one. That they believed in teamwork.

'And, of course, he's fresh meat,' the nurse said.

The receptionist laughed. 'Oh, Gem. Trust *you* to think of that.'

Ollie, who had just opened his mouth ready to say hello, stood there in silence, gobsmacked.

Fresh meat?

Right now, he was still smarting too much from the fallout from the wedding-that-wasn't to want any kind of relationship. And it rankled that someone was discussing him in that way. Fresh meat. A slab of beefcake. Clearly this 'Gem' woman made a habit of this, given the receptionist's comment.

Well, he'd just have to make sure she realised that she was barking up completely the wrong tree. And he didn't care if his metaphors were mixed.

He gave a loud cough. 'Good morning.'

'Oh! Good morning.' The receptionist smiled at him. 'We're not actually open yet, but can I help you?'

'I'm Oliver Langley,' he said.

The receptionist's cheeks went pink as she clearly realised that he'd overheard the end of their conversation.

Yeah. She might well be embarrassed. Fresh meat, indeed.

'I'm Maddie Jones, the receptionist—well, obviously,' she said. 'Welcome to the practice. Can I get you a cup of coffee, Dr Langley?'

'Thank you, but I'm fine,' he said coolly. 'I don't expect to be waited on.'

The nurse next to her also turned round to greet him.

'Good morning, Dr Langley. Nice to meet you,' she said with a smile.

Surely she must realise that he'd overheard what she'd just said about him? And yet she was still being all smiley and sparkly-eyed. Brazening it out? That didn't sit well with him at all.

'I'm Gemma Baxter,' she said. 'I'm one of the practice nurse practitioners. Caroline asked me to look after you this week, as she's away on holiday.'

'That's kind of you, Nurse Baxter,' he said, keeping his voice expressionless, 'but quite unnecessary.'

'Call me Gemma. And, if nothing else,' she said, 'I can at least show you where everything is in the surgery.' She disappeared for a moment, then came through to join him in the waiting area. 'It's pretty obvious that this is the waiting area,' she said, gesturing to the chairs. 'The nurses' and HCA's rooms are this side of Reception—' she gestured to the corridor to their left '—the pharmacy's through the double doors to the right, the patient toilets are over there in the corner, and the doctors' rooms are this side.'

She gestured to the other corridor. 'If you'd like to follow me? The staff toilets, the kitchen and rest room are here, behind Reception and the admin team.' She led him into the kitchen. 'Coffee, tea, hot chocolate and fruit tea are in the cupboard above the kettle, along with the mugs. The dishwasher's next to the fridge, and there's a rota for emptying it; and the microwave's self-explanatory. We all put a couple of pounds into the kitty every week and Maddie keeps the supplies topped up. If there's anything you want that isn't here, just let Maddie know.'

She smiled at him. 'I need to start checking the out-of-hours notifications and hospital letters before my triage calls and vaccination clinic this morning, so I'm going to leave you here. Your room's the third on the right, but obviously you'll see your name on the door anyway.'

'Thank you for the tour,' he said. That 'fresh meat' comment had rubbed him up the wrong way, but he was going to have to work with her for the next three months so it'd be sensible to be polite and make the best of it.

'I'll come and find you at lunchtime,' she said. 'As it's your first day, lunch is on me.'

'That's—' But he didn't have time to tell her that it was totally unnecessary and he'd sort out his own lunch, thanks all the same, because she'd already gone through to the other corridor.

Ollie made himself a coffee, then headed for his consulting room. It was a bright, airy space; there was a watercolour on the wall of a castle overlooking the sea, which he vaguely recognised as a local attraction. A desk; a couple of chairs for his patient and a parent or support person; and a computer. Everything neatly ordered and in its place; nothing personal.

He checked his phone for the username and password the practice administrator had sent him last week, logged on to the system and changed the password. Then he put an alarm on his phone to remind him when telephone triage started, and once his emails came up he started to work through the discharge summaries, hospital letters and referrals from over the weekend.

Gemma knew she was making a bit of a snap judgement—the sort of thing she normally disapproved of—but Oliver Langley seemed so closed-off. He hadn't responded to the warmth of her smile or her greeting, and he'd been positively chilly when she'd said she'd show him round. She sincerely hoped he'd be a bit warmer with their patients. When you were worried about your health, the last thing you needed was a doctor being snooty with you. You needed someone who'd listen and who'd reassure you.

Yes, sure, he was gorgeous: tall, with dark floppy hair and blue eyes, reminding her of a young Hugh Grant. But, when you were a medic, it didn't matter what you looked like; what mattered was how you behaved towards people. So far, from what Gemma had seen, Oliver Langley was very self-contained. If he was the best fit for the practice, as Caroline had claimed, Gemma hated to think what the other interviewees had been like. Robots, perhaps?

Hopefully she could work some kind of charm offensive on him over lunch. She intended to get a genuine smile out of him, even if she had to exhaust her entire stock of terrible jokes.

She took a gulp of the coffee she'd made earlier and checked the out-of-hours log, to see which of their patients had needed urgent treatment over the weekend and needed following up. Then she clicked onto the triage list Maddie had sent through, before starting her hour and a half of phone triage.

The system was one of the things the practice had kept from the Covid days. It was more efficient for dealing with minor illnesses and giving advice about coughs and colds and minor fevers; but in Gemma's view you could often tell a lot from a patient's body language—something that could prompt her to ask questions to unlock what her patient was *really* worrying about. That was something that telephone triage had taken away, since the Covid days. And trying to diagnose a rash or whether a wound had turned septic, from looking at a blurred photograph taken on a phone and sent in low resolution so it would actually reach the surgery email, had been next to impossible.

At least things were a bit easier now. They were all adjusting to the 'new normal'. She worked her way through the triage list until it was time to start her vaccination clinic. Even though the vaccination meant she had to make little ones cry, it also meant she got a chance for baby cuddles. Gemma would never admit to being broody, but if she was honest with herself her biological clock always sat up and took notice when she had this kind of clinic.

It had been twelve years since she'd lost her little sister—since she'd lost her entire family, because her parents had closed off, too, unable to deal with their loss. Gemma had been so desperate to feel loved and to stop the pain of missing Sarah that she'd chosen completely the wrong way to do it; she'd gone off the rails and slept with way too many boys. Once her best friend's mum had sat her down and talked some sense into her, Gemma had ended up going the other way: so determined not to be needy that she wouldn't let her boyfriends close, and the relationships had fizzled out within weeks. She'd never managed to find anyone she'd really clicked with.

So the chances of her attending this particular clinic rather than running it were looking more and more remote. It was a good six months since she'd last had a casual date, let alone anything more meaningful. The nearest she'd get to having a real family of her own was being godmother to Scarlett, her best friend's daughter. She was grateful for that, but at the same time she wondered why she still hadn't been able to fix her own family. Why she still couldn't get through to her parents.

She shook herself. Ridiculous. Why was she thinking about this now?

Perhaps, she thought, because Oliver Langley was precisely the sort of man she'd gone for, back in her difficult days. Tall, dark-haired, blue-eyed and gorgeous. And his coolness towards her had unsettled her; she was used to people reacting to her warmth and friendliness in kind.

Well, tough. It was his problem, not hers, and she didn't have time to worry about it now. She had a job to do. She went into the corridor and called her first patient for her clinic.

CHAPTER TWO

'I'VE BEEN DREADING this appointment. I really hate needles,' Fenella Nichols confessed as she sat down by Gemma's desk, settling the baby on her lap.

Gemma could've guessed that, because the year-old baby was fussing, having picked up on her mum's stress. 'A lot of people do,' she said with a smile. 'But you're doing absolutely the right thing, bringing Laura here to protect her. Meningitis is nasty stuff, and so are mumps and measles and rubella. And you've dressed her perfectly, so I've got easy access to her thigh and her arm and it won't cause her a lot of worry.' She stroked the baby's cheek. 'Hello, gorgeous. Do I get a smile?'

To her relief, the baby gurgled.

'You've got her red book?' Gemma checked.

'Yes.' Fenella produced it and put it on the desk.

'Great. How's everything going?' This was

the point where Gemma knew that if there were any real worries, Fenella would unburden herself and Gemma could start to fix things.

'My husband thinks she's a bit behind. I mean, I know she's a bit on the small side, but I thought she takes after me.'

Fenella was slender and just about five feet tall, a good six inches shorter than Gemma. 'You're probably right. I'll measure her and look at her centile chart,' Gemma promised. 'And I can hear for myself that she's starting to get chatty.'

'Dada, dog and duck are her favourite words,' Fenella said with a smile. 'And she's pulling herself up on the furniture.'

'It won't be long until she's walking, then. You'll be seeing the health visitor about her milestones,' Gemma said, 'but from what you're saying there's nothing to worry about.' Gemma waved at the baby, who waved back. Then she took a picture book from the tray on her desk, opened it and held it in front of the baby. 'Can you see the duck, Laura?'

The baby cooed and pointed at the picture of a duck.

'Can you help Laura find the lamb in the book, Fenella?'

With both mum and baby distracted, it was

easy for Gemma to prepare Laura's thigh for the vaccination and administer it. Laura cried for a moment, but was soon distracted by her mum turning the page to another picture. 'Dog!' she said, pointing.

'That's brilliant,' Gemma said. 'You might see a red area come up around the injection site later this morning, Fenella, but that'll go in a couple of days. And sometimes after the meningitis vaccine babies get a bit of a temperature, but I'm going to give Laura some liquid paracetamol now to help stop that happening. Make sure you give her plenty to drink, and if she feels a bit hot take off a layer or two. You can give her more paracetamol if you need to in four hours, and if you're worried give us a call.'

'All right. Thank you, Gemma.'

Gemma weighed and measured the baby, recording the figures as well as the vaccination details in the red book. 'Laura's following the same trend line she's been on since birth, a shade under the middle, so I'm very happy. Is there anything you're concerned about, or anything you'd like to chat over?'

'No.' Fenella smiled. 'But I think I'm going to make my husband bring her for the next injections.'

Gemma laughed. 'That sounds like a good plan.'

Her next patient was a little older, so she distracted him from the 'sharp scratch' by getting him to sing 'Old Macdonald Had a Zoo' with her.

'Zoo?' his mum asked, laughing.

'Absolutely,' Gemma said with a grin. 'It makes a change from a farm with cows and sheep. With a zoo, we can have elephants, tigers, lions, crocodiles...'

'Crocodiles!' the little boy said, his eyes going round with excitement.

'A snap-snap here,' Gemma sang.

In all the excitement of the song, the little boy forgot to be upset about the needle.

This was one of the bits of the job Gemma loved: the interaction with her younger patients. If she hadn't decided to go into general practice, she would definitely have worked in paediatrics.

She dispensed a sticker announcing 'I was THIS brave' at the end of the appointment, did the necessary cleaning in the treatment room, and called in her next patient. As it was the school holidays, she also had a couple of teenagers at the clinic who'd missed their meningitis vaccine and needed to catch up.

'So you're off to uni in a couple of months?' she asked the first one.

'*If* I get my grades.' Millie bit her lip. 'I'm dreading results day.'

'You have my sympathy. I still remember mine.' The second time round had given Gemma the grades she'd needed, but the first time had been a disaster. Her year of going off the rails had meant she'd failed her exams spectacularly and she'd had to repeat the second year of her A levels and resit her exams. 'Just remember that there's always a plan B,' Gemma said. 'Even if you don't get your first choice, you're still going to have a good time because you'll be doing the subject you love.'

'I guess.' Millie grimaced. 'Mum's worrying.'

'That's what mums do,' Gemma said. 'But this is one worry you can tick off her list.' She smiled. 'My mum was the same.' Well. Almost. After Sarah's death, her mum had seemed to close off. But her best friend Claire's mum Yvonne had worried about her. And Yvonne had been the one to sit down with Gemma and finally make her get her act together after she'd failed her exams. 'She got me to make a list of what I was worrying about. Then we talked about it and made a plan together. My mum—' well, Claire's mum '—worried about me eating properly, so I got her to teach me how to make some meals that were quick, easy and cheap.'

'That's a really good idea. Thank you,' Millie said.

'Good luck, and I hope you have a wonderful time at uni,' Gemma said when Millie left.

Her clinic finished on time; she sorted out her paperwork, checked on the practice app that Oliver's last appointment had finished, then went to knock on his door.

'Time for lunch,' she said, giving him her warmest smile in the hope that it might thaw him out a bit.

He looked up from his desk. 'Really, there's no need.'

He was going to be stubborn about it? Well, maybe he needed to learn that he wasn't the only one who could be stubborn. He might only be here temporarily, but for those three months he was going to be part of the team. Being snooty and refusing to mix with everyone wasn't an option. 'There's every need,' she said. 'You're new to the village and it's your first day at the practice. We're a team and we look after each other. I thought we could have lunch by the cliffs—the local bakery does the best sandwiches ever. And, as it's your first day, it's my shout.'

When he opened his mouth, she guessed he was about to refuse, and added swiftly, 'No protests allowed.' He looked wary, and she sighed. 'Look, it's just a sandwich and some coffee. A welcome-to-the-practice sort of thing. You're not under any obligation to me whatsoever if you accept.'

He looked awkward, then. 'Thank you,' he muttered.

She'd get a proper smile out of him if it killed her. 'I'm glad that's settled. It's a five-minute walk from here to the bakery, and five minutes from there to the cliffs.'

He followed her out of the door. Still silent, she noticed. OK. She'd start the conversation. Something easy. Food was always a safe subject. 'For the purposes of transparency, the bakery happens to be owned by my best friend, but I stand by what I said. Claire makes amazingly good sourdough and her brownies have to be tasted to be believed.'

'Right.'

Oh, for pity's sake. Could he not meet her halfway and at least make an *effort* at small talk? She tried again. 'Are you not a cake person?'

He wrinkled his nose. 'Not really.'

So he wouldn't be buying cake from her on her regular Friday morning bake sale. 'Looks as if we're opposites, then,' she said lightly, 'because I think cake makes the world go round.'

Was she being paranoid, or was he looking at her as if she had two heads? If she hadn't promised Caroline she'd look after him, she would've walked away and left him to his own grouchy company.

At the bakery, once they'd chosen their sandwiches and he'd ordered an espresso, she added a lemon and raspberry cake to their order along with one of Claire's savoury muffins.

Oliver carried the brown paper bag with their lunch, but he didn't make conversation on the steep path up to the cliffs.

Was he shy, perhaps? He might find it easier to be professional with his patients than with his coworkers, but somehow she was going to have to persuade him to thaw a little. They really didn't need any tension at work.

Finally they made it to the clifftop. Gemma took the picnic blanket from her backpack and spread it on the grass with a flourish. 'Have a seat,' she said with a smile.

'Do you always carry a picnic blanket?' he asked, looking surprised.

She nodded. 'If it's not raining, I usually come up here for lunch. The view's amazing.'

'It is,' he agreed, looking out at the sand and the sea.

'It's the best place I know to clear your head and set you up for the rest of the day.'

He sat down next to her, opened the paper bag, checked the labels written on the contents and handed her a coffee and a sandwich. 'Thank you for lunch.'

'You're welcome. How was your first morning?'

'Fine.'

He was still being cool. So much for hoping that lunch might win him round.

'Win me round?' The coolness was verging on arctic, now.

She grimaced. 'I said that aloud, didn't I? I'm sorry.' She took a deep breath. 'We don't seem to be getting on very well. I was trying to be nice and look out for a new colleague. If I've come across as in your face or patronising, I apologise.'

He was still looking at her as if she had two heads. She sighed inwardly. What would it take to get a decent working relationship going with her new colleague?

Then again, she hadn't managed to fix her relationship with her parents. She was the common factor in both situations, so maybe *she* was the problem. Maybe she should just give up—on both counts. 'Now I know you're not a cake person, I won't try to sell you a Friday Fundraiser cake.'

'What's a Friday Fundraiser cake?'

'Before Covid, I used to have a cake stall in the waiting room on Friday mornings to raise money for the local cardiac unit. I'd sell cake and cookies to patients, staff, anyone who happened to be around.' She sighed. 'Caroline's given me the go-ahead to do it again now, but it's on a much smaller scale because we don't have as many face-to-face appointments as we used to.' She shrugged.

'But it's better than nothing. All the little bits add up. I do a big fundraiser every three or four months; my skydive in the spring had to be postponed because of bad weather, so I'm doing it next month. There's no obligation to sponsor me, but if you'd like to then I'd be very grateful, even if it's only a pound.' She gave him a wry smile. 'I've been fundraising for about ten years, so I think everyone else in the practice has got donation fatigue, by now—if I'm honest, probably everyone in the village.'

Donation fatigue?

Ollie thought about it, and then the penny dropped.

'That's why you told Maddie I was fresh meat?'

She looked horrified. 'Oh, no! I mean—yes, I did say that, but the way you just said it makes it sound *terrible*. I'm so sorry. And I'm not...' She shook her head, her eyes widening as a thought clearly struck her. 'Oh, no. Did you think I was some kind of man-eater planning to hit on you?'

It had rather crossed his mind.

And he was pretty sure it showed on his face, because she said quickly, 'That's not who I am.' She bit her lip. 'I barely know you. You could be married with children, or at least involved with someone. Of course I wasn't sizing you up as a potential partner. No wonder you've been so reserved with me, thinking I was about to pounce on you. I'm really sorry.' She grimaced. 'What a horrible way to welcome you to the practice.'

Ollie looked at her. The dismay on her face seemed genuine.

'Look, forget what I just said about asking you to sponsor me,' she said. 'I know they say there's no such thing as a free lunch, but this really *is* one. I just wanted to do what Caroline asked of me and welcome you to the practice. To show you where the best place is to grab a sandwich, even if I am a tiny bit biased, and somewhere nice to sit and eat or even just walk for a bit if you need to clear your head, because when you're new to the area it's always good to have someone showing you these things.'

Even though Ollie didn't quite trust his own judgement any more—not after he'd got it so wrong with Tabby, thinking that she'd loved him as much as he'd loved her—the look in Gemma's eyes seemed genuine. And she seemed to be trying very hard to hold out an olive branch. Maybe he should do the same.

'I think we got off on completely the wrong foot,' he said. 'Let's start again. I'm Oliver Langley and I'm the locum for Aadya Devi, for the next three months.' He held out his hand.

'Gemma Baxter, nurse practitioner,' she said, taking his hand and shaking it. 'Welcome to Ashermouth Bay Surgery, Dr Langley.'

Shaking her hand was a mistake, Ollie realised quickly. His fingers tingled at her touch and adrenalin pumped through him, making his heart start to pound. He couldn't remember the last time he'd been this aware of anyone, even Tabby, and he couldn't quite let himself meet Gemma's eyes. 'Thank you,' he muttered, dropping her hand again.

'Caroline said you were from London. What made you decide to come to Northumberland?'

To escape the fallout of his bad decisions. To hide and lick his wounds. To be a living donor for his twin's kidney transplant. Not that he planned to explain any of that. Even though he knew it wasn't the real reason why, he said, 'My parents moved up here ten years ago. Dad developed angina, and Mum wanted him to retire early and take things a bit easier. So they spend their days pottering around in the garden and going out for lunch.'

'Sounds nice,' she said. 'And they must be so pleased that you'll be closer to them now than you were in London.'

And his twin, but Ollie wasn't quite ready to share that yet. 'What about you?' he asked. 'Are you from round here?'

'Yes. I grew up in Ashermouth Bay. I did my training in Liverpool, but I knew I wanted to work back here,' she said. 'Luckily, when I qualified, one of the nurses at the practice was thinking about retiring, so I had the chance to work here and do my nurse practitioner training part-time.'

'So your family lives here?'

A shadow seemed to pass across her face, or maybe he was imagining it, but then she said, 'Not far from here.'

'And you always wanted to work in general practice rather than at the hospital?'

She nodded. 'I like the idea of really knowing my patients, watching them grow up and looking after their whole families. Being part of a community—in a hospital, you might look after someone for a few days or a few weeks, but it isn't the same.' She looked at him. 'Did you always plan to be a GP?'

'I nearly went into obstetrics,' he said. 'I trained in London. I enjoyed all my rotations, and delivering babies was amazing. But then my dad was diagnosed with angina, and it made me have a rethink.'

'You weren't tempted to specialise in cardiology?'

He shook his head. 'Partly because it was a little bit too close to the bone. But I realised I wanted to be the kind of doctor who'd be able to pick up a problem before his patient really started to suffer from it. Which meant being a GP.'

'Good plan,' she said.

He finished his sandwich. 'You were right. This bread's as good as any I've eaten in a posh café in London.'

'Wait until you try the muffin,' she said. 'I know you're not a cake person, but this is savoury.' She rummaged in the brown paper bag and brought out a wrapped muffin. 'Your challenge, should you accept it, is to tell me what's in the muffin.'

He liked the slightly teasing look in her eyes. And he was shocked to realise that, actually, he liked *her*.

'So what's in it?' she tested.

'Spices and cheese,' he said.

She gave him a mock-sorrowful look. 'That's much too general.'

'Remember what the G in GP stands for,' he retorted.

She laughed, and it made her light up from the inside. Her dark eyes sparkled and there was an almost irresistible curve to her mouth. And Ollie found himself staring at Gemma Baxter, spellbound, for a moment.

He really hadn't expected this.

It was nearly four months since he'd split up with Tabby. Although he knew he had to move on, he hadn't really noticed any other women since then. Until today: and he really wasn't sure he was ready for this right now.

He needed to backtrack, fast, before he said something stupid. He didn't want to let Gemma close; yet, at the same time, he didn't want to freeze her out. He'd thought Gemma was the careless type when he'd first met her, but he was beginning to realise that there was more to her than that. Someone careless wouldn't be doing a skydive for charity.

The best compromise would be to stick to a safe subject. 'So tell me about Ashermouth Bay.'

'What do you want to know?' she asked. 'About the sort of things that are popular with tourists, or a potted history of the town?'

'A bit of both,' he said.

'OK. Ashermouth Bay used to be a fishing village,' she said. 'Obviously times change, and now the town's more reliant on tourism than on fishing. Though you can still take a boat trip out to see the puffins on the islands offshore, and if you're lucky you might see dolphins and porpoises on the way. There's a colony of seals nearby, too, and they tend to come into the bay when the pups are born—which is basically about now. If walking's your thing, you can walk right along the bay at low tide and go up to the castle; and you can see a bit of an old shipwreck along the way.'

'That's just the sort of thing I would've loved as a kid,' he said.

'The local history group does a ghost walk

once a month in the village,' she said, 'with tales of smugglers and pirates. If castles are your thing, there are loads of them nearby—though I'm guessing, as you said your parents live near here, you already know all about them.'

'My mum loves visiting stately homes for the gardens,' he said. 'And I've driven her and Dad to a few when I've come to visit.'

'If you like sport, the village has a cricket team and a football team,' she said. 'And there's an adventure centre based in the harbour if you want to do surfing, paddle-boarding, kite-surfing and the like.'

All things Ollie knew his brother would adore; out of the two of them, Rob was the adrenalin junkie. It was why his twin worked in a fast-paced emergency department in Manchester, was a member of the local mountain rescue team as well as enjoying climbing on his days off, and spent his holidays working for a humanitarian aid organisation. Ollie adored his brother, but he was happy being grounded rather than pushing himself to take extra risks, the way Rob did. The family joke was that Ollie had Rob's share of being sensible and Rob had Ollie's share of being adventurous. 'The cliffs and the beach sound just fine to me,' he said.

She glanced at her watch. 'We need to be heading back.'

'Admin and phone calls before afternoon surgery?' he asked.

'Absolutely.' She smiled at him.

'Thank you for lunch,' he said.

'You're very welcome.'

'Let me help you fold the blanket.' Though when his fingers accidentally brushed against hers, again he felt the prickle of adrenalin down his spine.

Ridiculous.

They were colleagues. He wasn't looking for a relationship. There were a dozen reasons why he shouldn't even think about what it might be like to kiss Gemma Baxter.

But he'd noticed the curve of her mouth, the fullness of her lower lip. And he couldn't help wondering.

He shook himself. They were colleagues, and nothing more. And he needed to make some kind of small talk on the way back to the practice, to make sure she didn't have a clue about the thoughts running through his head.

Once he'd thawed out a little, Oliver Langley had turned out to be surprisingly nice, Gemma thought. Maybe he was right and they'd just got off on the wrong foot. And Caroline had said she'd thought he'd fit in well with the team.

The one thing that shocked her, though, was when Oliver had finally given her a genuine smile. It had completely transformed his face, turning him from that cool, austere stranger into someone absolutely gorgeous. His smile had made her heart beat a little bit too quickly for her liking.

She couldn't afford to let herself be attracted to their new locum. Quite apart from the fact that he might already be involved with someone else, she didn't have a great track record. Even if you ignored that year of disastrous relationships and the following two years of not dating anyone at all while she concentrated on getting through her exams and putting herself back together, her love life ever since had been hopeless. All her relationships had fizzled out within a few weeks. She'd never met anyone that she'd felt really connected to, someone she really wanted to share her life with.

Claire, her best friend, had a theory that it was because Gemma was so terrified of being needy and clingy, she went too far the other way and wouldn't actually let anyone in.

But it wasn't about being needy or clingy.

It was about trust. She'd loved her little sister and her parents. But her parents had shut off from her after Sarah's death, lost in their grief, and Gemma had never been able to connect with them since. And maybe that was what was still holding her back, even after she'd had counselling: if she really loved someone and let them close, what if it all went wrong, the way it had with her parents, and they left her?

So it was easier to keep her relationships short and sweet and avoid that risk completely. Make sure she was the one to leave, not them.

Gemma's afternoon was a busy mixture of triage calls and surgery; after she'd finished writing up the notes from her last patient, she changed out of her uniform and drove to her parents' house for her monthly duty visit. She wasn't giving up on them, the way they'd given up on her. One day, she'd manage to get her family back. She just had to find the right key to unlock their hearts.

'Aadya's locum started at the surgery today,' she said brightly.

'Oh,' her mum said.

'He seems nice.'

'That's good,' her dad said.

The silence stretched out painfully until Gemma couldn't take any more. 'Shall I make us a cup of tea?' she suggested.

'If you like, love,' her mum said.

Putting the kettle on and sorting out mugs gave her five minutes of respite to think up some new topics of conversation. What her parents had been doing in the garden; the puppy Maddie was getting in a couple of weeks; how much sponsorship money she'd raised so far for the skydive. But it was such a struggle, when they gave anodyne responses every time. Her parents were the only people she knew who always gave a closed answer to an open question.

How very different it was when she dropped in to see Claire's mum. There was never any awkwardness or not knowing what to say next. Yvonne always greeted her with a hug, asked her how her day was, and chatted to her about the classes she ran in the craft shop next to Claire's bakery. Gemma had tried to persuade her own mum to go along to a class, thinking that she might enjoy the embroidery class or knitting, but she'd always been gently but firmly rebuffed. Her parents simply couldn't bear to come back to the village they'd lived in when Sarah died; they visited once a month to put flowers on their daughter's grave, but that was as much as they could manage.

And they'd never, ever visited Gemma's flat. She knew it was because they found it hard to face all the might-have-beens, but it still felt like another layer of rejection.

After another hour of struggling to get her parents to talk to her, she did the washing up, kissed both parents' cheeks, and drove home. Feeling too miserable to eat dinner, and knowing that a walk and the sound of the sea swishing against the shore would lift her mood, she headed to the beach to watch the changing colours in the sky.

One day she'd break through to her parents again. And then she'd have the confidence to find someone to share her life with—someone who wouldn't abandon her when things got tough—and it would ease the loneliness.

But for now she'd focus on how lucky she was. She had good friends, a job she loved, and she lived in one of the nicest bits of the world. Maybe wanting more—wanting love—was just too greedy.

Ollie arrived home to find a note through his front door saying that a parcel had been delivered to his neighbour.

When he'd collected it, he didn't need to

look at the card that came with it; only one person would send him a mini-hamper with seriously good cheese, olives, oatmeal crackers, and a bottle of good red wine. But he opened the card anyway.

Hope your first day was great. If it wasn't, you have my permission to scoff all the cheese. Otherwise, you'd better save me some for Thursday night or there will be Big Trouble.
R

He rang his twin. 'Thank you for the parcel.'

'My pleasure. It always made my day when I had a parcel in hospital, and I think a first day anywhere deserves a parcel.' The smile in Rob's voice was obvious. 'So how did it go?'

'OK,' Ollie said.

'Your colleagues are all nice?'

'Yeah. Though I got off on the wrong foot with the nurse practitioner, to start with.' Ollie explained his clash with Gemma.

'Olls, I know Tabby hurt you—but don't let that change the way you respond to anyone with two X chromosomes,' Rob said softly.

'I'm not responding at all. I'm not looking to get involved with anyone. It's only been three and a half months since Tabby cancelled the wedding.'

'I'm not telling you to rush in and sweep the next woman you meet off her feet. Just don't close yourself off from potential happiness, that's all,' Rob advised.

'Mmm,' Ollie said, not wanting to fight with his twin. But thinking about Gemma Baxter unsettled him. That spark of attraction between them on the cliffs, when their hands had touched—he really hadn't expected that. This three-month locum job was meant to give himself the space to get his head straight again. Starting a new relationship really wasn't a good idea.

'Be kind to yourself, Olls,' Rob said. 'And I'll see you on Thursday.'

CHAPTER THREE

THE NEXT MORNING, when Gemma walked into the staff kitchen at the surgery, Oliver was already there.

'Good morning. The kettle's hot,' he said, indicating his mug. 'Can I make you a drink?'

'Thank you. Coffee, with milk and no sugar, please,' she said, smiling back.

He gave her another of those smiles that made her pulse rocket, and she had to remind herself sharply that Oliver was her new colleague and off limits. Yes, he was attractive; but that didn't mean he was available.

After her triage calls that morning, Gemma was booked in for her weekly visit to the nursing home, where she was able to assess any particular resident the manager was concerned about, and carried on with their rolling programme of six-monthly wellbeing reviews to check every resident's care plan and medication needs. Her path didn't cross with Oliver's again that day, and she was cross with herself for being disappointed. 'He's your colleague. No more, no less,' she reminded herself yet again.

At least she had her Tuesday dance aerobics class with Claire to take her mind off it. Or so she'd thought.

'Your lunch date, yesterday,' Claire said. 'He looked nice.'

'He's my colleague—Aadya's locum,' Gemma said. 'And it wasn't a lunch date. Caroline asked me to help him settle in, that's all.'

'You went very pink when he said something to you in the bakery,' Claire said. 'And he looks like your type.'

Gemma gave her a wry smile. 'For all I know, he's already involved with someone. We're just colleagues.'

'Hmm. Talking of colleagues, Andy's got a new colleague. He's single, and our age,' Claire said. 'Maybe you could both come over to dinner at the weekend.'

Gemma hugged her. 'Love you, Claire-bear, but I really don't need you to find me a partner. I'm fine just as I am.'

Though they both knew she wasn't quite telling the truth.

* * *

On Wednesday morning, Gemma had an asthma clinic, and her first patient was booked in for a series of spirometry tests. Samantha was forty years old and a smoker, and had persistent breathlessness and a cough. Although at the last appointment Sam had said that she thought her cough was just a smoker's cough, she'd also admitted that she seemed to get more and more chest infections over the winter and had started wheezing when she walked up the hill, so Gemma wanted to check if there was another lung condition such as asthma or COPD that was making Sam's breathlessness worse.

'This is going to help us get to the bottom of your breathlessness and your cough, Sam,' she said, 'so we can get you the right treatment to help you. Just to remind you what I said at the last appointment, I'm going to test your breathing through a spirometer to get a baseline, then give you some asthma medication, get you to sit in the waiting room while the medication takes effect, and run the test again to see if the medication makes a difference.'

'I remembered to wear loose, comfortable clothing, like you said,' Sam said. 'I didn't have even a single glass of wine last night, and I haven't smoked for twenty-four hours. It was murder, last night—I really wanted just a quick cigarette—but Marty wouldn't let me.'

'Good,' Gemma said with a smile. 'How are your headaches?'

'Not great,' Sam admitted. 'Do you think they're something to do with my breathlessness?'

'Very possibly,' Gemma said. 'Now, I just want to run through a checklist to make sure there isn't anything else that might affect the results.' She ran through the list with Sam, and to her relief there was nothing else.

'Great. We're ready to start. Are you sitting comfortably?'

Sam nodded.

'This is how I want you to breathe into the spirometer,' Gemma said, and demonstrated. 'I want you to breathe in and completely fill your lungs with air, close your lips tightly round the mouthpiece, and then blow very hard and fast. We'll do that three times, and then a test where I want you to keep blowing until your lungs are completely empty. I'll put a very soft clip on your nose to make sure all the air goes into the mouthpiece when you breathe out. Is that OK?'

Sam nodded, and Gemma encouraged her through the tests.

'Well done, that's brilliant,' she said. 'Now I'm going to get you to take some asthma medication, and I'd like you to sit in the waiting room for about twenty minutes so it has a chance to open up your airways; then we'll repeat the test and compare the results to each other.'

'My mouth's a bit dry,' Sam said.

'It's fine to have a drink of water while you're waiting,' Gemma said.

'Just not a cigarette?' Sam asked wryly.

'Exactly.'

Gemma helped Sam to take the asthma medication, then saw her next patient for an asthma review while Sam's medication took effect.

'How are you feeling?' she asked when Sam came back into the room. 'Has the medication made it easier to breathe?'

'A bit,' Sam said.

'That's good.'

Once Gemma had done the second set of tests, she compared the two sets of graphs. 'I'd just like to run these past one of the doctors first, if you don't mind?' she said.

'Sure. Do you want me to go back to the waiting room?' Sam asked.

'No, it's fine to wait here. He'll be here in a minute.' According to the roster, Oliver was the duty doctor this morning and was doing phone triage right now. Gemma sent him a note over the practice messaging system.

Before your next call, please can we have a quick word about one of my patients? Did spirometry, but patient not responded as well as I hoped to bronchodilator meds—think we're looking at COPD but would appreciate a second opinion.

Within seconds, a message flashed back.

Good timing—just finished call. Coming now.

Gemma opened the door at his knock.

'Sam, this is Dr Langley, who's working here while Dr Devi's on maternity leave,' she said. 'Dr Langley, this is Sam.' She gave him a potted version of Sam's patient history.

'Nice to meet you, Sam,' Oliver said. 'So may I look at the graphs?'

Gemma handed them over, and he checked them swiftly. 'I agree with you,' he said quietly.

'Sam, this is what a normal pattern of breathing looks like for someone of your height, age, sex and ethnic group,' Gemma said, showing

Sam the graph on her computer. 'And this is your pattern.'

'So I'm not breathing out enough air,' Sam said.

'Instead of you blowing most of the air out of your lungs in the first second, there's a shallower curve,' Oliver said. 'It's what we call an obstructive pattern, meaning that you've got a lung condition which narrows your airways, so the air is flowing out more slowly than it should.'

'I was hoping that the medication would open up your airways a lot more, so your pattern would match that of someone who doesn't have a lung condition, and that would've meant I'd diagnose you with asthma,' Gemma said, 'but unfortunately it hasn't. There are some other conditions that can cause breathlessness, so I'm going to send you for a chest X-ray and do some blood tests to check if you're anaemic, or if there's a higher than average concentration of red blood cells in your blood.'

'Chest X-ray?' Sam went white. 'Oh, no. Are you telling me you think I've got lung cancer?'

'I'm just being thorough and ruling things out,' Gemma said. 'From the look of this graph, I think you have something called chronic obstructive pulmonary disease—COPD for short.'

'I agree with Nurse Practitioner Baxter. Chronic means it's long-term and won't go away, obstructive means your airways are narrowed so it's harder for you to breathe out quickly and air gets trapped in your chest, and pulmonary means it affects your lungs,' Oliver added.

Sam grimaced. 'And I've got it because I'm a smoker?'

'We're not judging you, but yes. Nine out of ten cases of COPD are caused by smoking,' Gemma said.

'Though COPD can also run in families,' Oliver said. 'And if you work in a place where you're exposed to a lot of dust, fumes or chemicals, that can contribute.'

'Nobody else in my family gets breathless, and I work in a garden centre. So it has to be the smoking,' Sam said with a sigh. 'I know I shouldn't do it. But I started smoking when I was fifteen, because all my friends were doing it and I didn't want to be left out. And then it got to be a habit. It calms me down when things get tough.

'I've tried to give up a couple of times, and I managed it when I was pregnant because I didn't want it to affect the baby, but Louisa's toddler tantrums sent me right back to having a quick cigarette in the garden to help calm me down, and I never managed to stop again.' She shook her head and grimaced. 'It's just too hard.'

'COPD isn't a condition we can cure, or even reverse,' Gemma said. 'But the best way to stop it getting any worse is for you to stop smoking.'

'We can support you,' Oliver said. 'There are lots of things that can help you—patches and gums and sprays. And you're three times more likely to be able to give up with our support than if you're struggling on your own.'

'We can also refer you for a pulmonary rehabilitation programme,' Gemma said. 'It's a six-week course with other people who have the same condition as you do. Some of the sessions will teach you exercises to help your breathing, but the trainer will also be able to teach you breathing techniques, how to manage stress, and how to manage your condition better.'

'That sounds good,' Sam said.

'We ask all our patients who have asthma or COPD to have a flu jab every year,' Gemma said, 'because when you have a lung condition you're more vulnerable to catching the flu in the first place, and developing complications.'

'And there's a one-off pneumococcal vaccine, which will help protect you against pneumonia,' Oliver added. 'I know it's a lot to take in, and it sounds scary, but we can help you.'

'You'll get a letter so you can book onto the pulmonary rehab course at a time that works for you,' Gemma said, 'and I'll refer you to a counsellor who can help you stop smoking. Plus you'll have regular appointments with me to see how you're doing, and to check that your symptoms are under control and you're not getting any side effects from the medication.'

'Thank you,' Sam said. 'And I'll try really hard to stop smoking. Really, I will.'

'You're not on your own,' Oliver said. 'That's the main thing. We're here to help.'

Once Sam and Oliver had left her consulting room, Gemma took a sip of water. Now she'd seen Oliver Langley with a patient, she could see exactly why the head of the practice had offered him the job. He was kind, supportive and clear without being patronising; he hadn't judged Sam for smoking; and he was a world away from the cold, slightly haughty man she'd first met on Monday morning. The way he'd worked with Gemma, backing her up, had made her feel as if she'd worked with him for years, rather than today being only his third day on the team.

But Oliver was still practically a stranger. And she needed to be sensible instead of noticing how her heart skipped a beat every time he smiled.

She sent him a note across the practice messaging system after she'd written up the notes and before seeing her next patient.

Thanks for your help with Sam's COPD. Appreciated.

You're welcome, he replied.

Gemma liked the fact that he had nice manners. The more she got to know Oliver Langley, the more she liked him.

Strictly as a colleague, she reminded herself, and saw her next patient.

Just when she'd seen her last appointment of morning surgery, her computer pinged with a message.

Are you busy for lunch, or can I buy you a sandwich and we can maybe sit on the cliffs again?

Which sounded as if they were about to start becoming friends.

She messaged back.

A sandwich would be nice. Thank you. Just writing up my last set of notes and I'll be with you.

Crazy.

Ollie knew he shouldn't be looking forward to lunch with Gemma.

But he was. He'd liked the way she'd been with her patient this morning, all calm and kind and reassuring. And the fact that she'd checked with him on a case she wasn't sure about: her patients' welfare came before her professional pride, which was exactly how it should be.

Gemma Baxter was nothing like the man-eater he'd assumed she was when he'd first set foot in the reception area on Monday morning and overheard that comment.

She was *nice*. Genuine.

And if Rob was here right now he'd grin and say that Gemma was just Ollie's type, with those huge eyes and all that fair hair.

He didn't need a type. This was a burgeoning friendship, that was all—and that was fine by him.

Once they'd chosen sandwiches and headed up to the cliffs, he helped her spread out the picnic blanket. Again, his fingers accidentally touched hers and it felt as if lightning zinged through him. His lower lip tingled, and he couldn't help moistening it with the tip of his tongue.

Oh, for pity's sake. He really needed to get a grip. Work, he thought. That was a safe subject. 'How was your morning?' he asked.

'Pretty good. Thanks for your help with Sam—I've only just taken over the practice asthma clinic, so I'm still finding my feet a bit.'

'No problem. That's what I'm here for,' he said.

'How was your morning?' she asked.

'Pretty good.' He smiled at her. 'I've been thinking. I'd like to sponsor you for your skydive. You said it was next month?'

'Two weeks on Friday,' she said. 'I have to admit, I'm feeling a bit nervous about it now. It's a tandem skydive, so I know I'm going to be perfectly safe with an instructor, but even the idea of stepping out of that plane makes my palms go sweaty.'

'You're clearly not scared of heights, though, or you wouldn't be here on the cliff.'

'No, but I wouldn't choose to go rock-climbing.' She looked at him. 'Though, actually, I guess that could be a potential challenge for the future. Maybe next year.'

He frowned. 'So why are you doing the skydive? I know you said it was for charity, but is it because you're challenging yourself to overcome your fears as well?'

'No, but people get bored of sponsoring the same thing. A skydive's good for raising the profile of the cause, too. There's a good chance it'll go on the local newspaper's website, along with my fundraising page details, so maybe people who don't know me but want to support the cause will donate something.'

'You said you were raising funds for the local hospital's cardiac unit. Is that because you did some of your training there?' he asked.

'No.' She took a deep breath, as if psyching herself up to say something. 'My little sister spent a while there. I'm fundraising in her memory.'

In her memory... Gemma's little sister had *died*?

Before he could process that, she said, 'It was a long time ago now. I caught a bug at school, and Sarah caught it from me. I got better, but she didn't—she was still breathless and struggling. The next thing we knew, she was in the cardiac unit, being diagnosed with myocarditis.'

He'd noticed exactly what she'd said. 'It wasn't your fault. If the bug was going round at school, she could've caught it from one of her friends, not just from you.'

'Uh-huh.'

It sounded as if she still blamed herself, even though as a medic she'd know that wasn't fair. 'Was she on the list for a transplant?' he asked.

'Yes, but we were waiting for months. The right donor just didn't come along.' She looked away. 'Sarah died when I was seventeen and she was thirteen.'

He reached over and squeezed her hand. 'I'm sorry. That must have been devastating for you and your family.'

'It was,' she admitted. 'I've had twelve years to get used to it, but I still miss my little sister. And I really didn't cope very well at the time.' She shrugged. 'This is why I do the fundraising. It won't bring my little sister back and it won't do anything for the donor lists, but the hospital is doing research into permanent artificial hearts. And if that works out, it means another family might not have to lose someone they love dearly.'

'I'm sorry I've brought back bad memories for you.'

'I have a lot of good memories of Sarah.' She smiled, though her eyes were suspiciously shiny and he rather thought she was holding back tears. 'Doing her hair and make-up for a school disco, painting her nails, making cakes with her, playing in the garden.'

Obviously her memories were what carried her through the tough times. 'I'll definitely sponsor you,' he said.

She shook her head. 'I don't want you to feel obliged. It's fine.'

He knew the way to persuade her to accept his offer. 'It's not that I feel obliged,' he said. 'I was very nearly in your shoes, earlier this year.'

Apart from the people in the support group she'd gone to—and that hadn't lasted for long—Gemma had never met anyone else who'd had someone close who needed a heart transplant. 'Someone in your family needed a heart transplant?'

'No. My brother needed a kidney transplant.'

She winced. 'That must've been hard for you all.'

He nodded. 'Rob's a bit of a thrill-seeker.

He's an A and E doctor in Manchester. He spends all his free time climbing, and he's on the local mountain rescue team. He took a six-month sabbatical to work with a humanitarian aid agency; he'd gone out to help with a region that had just been hit by an earthquake. He had stomach pains when he'd been there for a couple of days, but he just assumed it was an ordinary tummy upset because he wasn't used to the food and water. And then, when he collapsed, they realised he had acute appendicitis.'

'Poor man—that's really tough.'

'It was. He was airlifted to a hospital, but his appendix burst on the way and he ended up with severe blood poisoning.' Oliver looked grim. 'It wiped out his kidneys, and he was on dialysis for a while.'

'But you got a donor?'

Oliver inclined his head. 'That's the main reason why I came back to Northumbria. We've been recuperating at our parents' house since the transplant.'

She blinked. '*We*—you mean, you were a living donor?'

'It was the obvious solution,' Oliver said. 'Rob's my twin.'

She hadn't expected that. 'Identical?'

'Apparently you can look identical but not actually be identical, so we had to do gene sequencing to check,' Oliver said. 'We're not quite identical. But, even so, getting a kidney from me meant his body was much less likely to reject it, and he's on a lower dose of immunosuppressant drugs than he'd need if anyone else had donated the kidney.'

'So that's why you're working up here now?'

'I was getting a bit stir-crazy,' he said. 'Mum's overdoing the cotton wool treatment.'

Gemma's parents had been too hurt to wrap her in cotton wool. Instead, they'd let their grief build a wall between them and never let her back in. She pushed the thought away.

'I'm the sensible one and it's been driving *me* crazy, so poor Rob is really having to learn to be patient.' He grinned. 'Which will probably do him good.'

'You're both so lucky,' she said. 'Your twin, because he has you; and you, because you could actually do something practical to help.'

'Yes. If it had been a different organ that failed, we would've had to wait for one to become available.' He wrinkled his nose. 'You know yourself, it's not very nice, waiting for someone else to die.'

'No. It'd feel horrible, knowing your loved

one's only still with you because someone else lost someone they loved,' Gemma said. 'Though Sarah thought about that, even when we knew it was too late and she was too ill for a transplant to work. She said she'd rather help someone else, even though she couldn't be helped, so she made our parents sign to donate everything that she could.'

'Brave kid,' Oliver said.

'She was. I wish…' Her breath hitched, and he could guess what she was thinking. She wished her sister hadn't died. Wished she'd been the one to be ill, to save her sibling. All the thoughts that had scrambled through his own brain in the early hours of the morning, when he couldn't sleep for thinking of what might have been.

'I often wonder what she would've been doing now,' Gemma said. 'She would've been twenty-five. I think she would've done something with art—she was really good.'

Oliver reached over and squeezed her hand. 'I'm sorry. I know how bad I felt when I thought I was going to lose Rob, earlier this year. It must've been so hard for you.'

'It was,' she agreed. 'And my parents have never recovered from it. They moved from the village, the year after Sarah died, because they couldn't handle all the memories.'

'You said you were seventeen at the time, so I assume they waited for you to finish your A levels before they moved?' he asked.

She shook her head. 'I made a complete mess of my exams and ended up having to resit them. But I didn't have to change schools; my best friend's mum let me stay with them and redo the year.' Yvonne had got her back on the straight and narrow. She'd *cared*. Been the stand-in mum Gemma had desperately needed.

'That's an amazing thing to do for someone,' he said.

'It is, and I'll always be grateful to her. Actually, I've been thinking lately that maybe I could offer a place for a teenager needing support—kind of pay forward what Claire's parents did for me. I live alone, but my working hours are regular so I could be there for someone who needed it.'

Gemma lived alone, and it sounded as if she didn't have a partner.

That really shouldn't make Ollie feel as pleased as it did. He wasn't looking for a relationship and, since Tabby had broken their engagement, he wasn't sure he'd be enough for anyone in any case.

But there was something about Gemma Baxter that drew him. A brightness, a warmth.

She'd come through the kind of nightmare that he'd dreaded happening to Rob and had kept him awake at night for months, and she was doing her best to try to stop other people having to go through it.

No partner.

He really needed to stop this. Yes, he liked Gemma and he was drawn to her. But he wasn't ready to move on with his life. He needed to be fair to her; all he could offer her right now was friendship.

'It'd be a good thing to do,' he agreed. 'Rewarding. You'd know you were really making a difference to someone's life.'

'So how's your brother doing now?' she asked.

'He's recovering well, but it's driving him a bit crazy not being at work. He knows there's no way he can go back out to do the humanitarian aid stuff or the mountain rescue—with only one working kidney, he's too much of a risk to be on a team. And he's not fit enough to go climbing again, either. He needs to be patient for a bit longer. And, for Rob, "rest" is most definitely a four-letter word.'

'So when did it all happen?' she asked.

'He collapsed at the beginning of March.

We did the transplant at the beginning of June, and I got the green light from the surgical team a couple of weeks ago to go back to work.'

'So you're still healing from donating the kidney, really.'

'I'm fine. It means no heavy lifting,' Ollie said, 'but that's about all. Luckily there weren't any complications for either of us, though Rob's not pleased that they've told him to wait a few more weeks before he goes back.'

'That's such an amazing thing to do, being a live donor and giving your brother a kidney.'

'I'm guessing you would've done the same for your sister.'

'Of course I would,' she said. 'Any live donation—a whole kidney, a piece of liver or a bit of pancreas. If I could've saved her...' Her eyes were suspiciously glittery.

'I know how lucky we were,' he said quietly. 'I had the chance to make a difference. And Rob's doing OK.'

'I'm glad.'

Ollie almost asked her to join them both for dinner, the following evening, but he didn't want his twin getting the wrong idea. 'Me, too.' He glanced at his watch. 'I guess we need to be getting back.'

'We do. I meant to mention this earlier, but are you busy on Friday evening?'

No, but he wasn't going to commit himself to anything until he knew what she had in mind. 'Why?'

'There's a pub quiz at The Anchor,' she explained. 'We normally field a team from the surgery. It starts at eight, but we've got a table booked to eat beforehand, if you'd like to join us.'

He really appreciated the fact she was trying to include him. 'Thank you. I'd love to.' He'd planned to spend Sunday with his family, but on Friday evening and Saturday he hadn't really been sure what to do with himself. It would be good to get to know his team a bit better.

'Great. Our table's booked for half-past six. The menu's small but I'd recommend absolutely everything on it. Everything's sourced as locally as possible.'

'Sounds good,' Ollie said. 'Count me in.' He took his phone from his pocket. 'What's your number? I'll text you so you'll have mine. And then you can text me back with the link to your fundraising page.'

'Thanks.' She recited her number, and he tapped it into his phone and sent her a text; a few seconds later, he heard a 'ping'.

'Got it,' she said.

And funny how her smile made the bright, sunny day feel even more sparkly.

CHAPTER FOUR

ON THURSDAY, OLLIE didn't see Gemma at the practice; according to Maddie, Gemma usually had Thursdays off. But he enjoyed showing his twin round the village that evening after dinner.

'What a view,' Rob said from the cliffs. 'I can see why you moved here, Olls. And you said they do kite-surfing in the bay? Fantastic. When can I book a session?'

Ollie cuffed his arm. 'No adventure stuff until your consultant says it's OK.'

'Just one tiny little session?' Rob wheedled. 'Half an hour—thirty teeny, tiny minutes?'

Ollie shook his head. 'Nope. And if you won't listen to me, I might have to casually mention to Mum that Rob the Risk-Taker is back.'

Rob groaned. 'Please don't. You know I love Mum dearly, and I know that she and Dad were worried sick about me when I was ill, but I really can't take much more of the cotton wool treatment. Neither could you,' he pointed out, 'or you wouldn't have escaped here.'

'True,' Ollie admitted.

'I want to escape, too. I've got an interview next week.'

Ollie stared at his twin in surprise. 'You're going back to Manchester already?'

'No. It's local—the hospital down the road. You know I'd taken that six months off to join the humanitarian aid team; as I've spent most of that time stuck in hospital or recovering, my boss has agreed to extend my sabbatical.'

Ollie felt his eyes widen. 'Please tell me you're not going back to an earthquake zone or what have you.'

'No. Apart from the fact that I have a gazillion hospital appointments, even I'm not that stupid,' Rob said. 'I'm hoping to get a part-time post at the hospital here for the next few months, until my consultant's happy with my recovery.'

'And then you'll go back to Manchester?'

'Yes. I'm desperate to go climbing again,' Rob said, 'but I promise I'm not going to do anything that will set my recovery back.'

'I'm glad to hear it,' Ollie said dryly. 'Though I'm not entirely convinced.'

'Seriously, Olls. If I have a setback, I'll be stuck sitting around recovering for even longer. That's not going to help my itchy feet. I don't want to give Mum more excuses to smother me. And, most importantly, I don't want to worry Dad to the point where his angina flares up,' Rob said. 'I couldn't live with myself if he got ill again because of me.'

'Now *that*,' Ollie said, 'convinces me.'

'Good.' Rob smiled. 'So how are you getting on with your nurse practitioner?'

'I'm getting on fine with all my colleagues,' Ollie said.

'Meaning you like her and you don't want to admit it.'

'She's my colleague, Rob. My *temporary* colleague. It's not a great idea. If we get together and it goes wrong, it'll be awkward at work. We're just going to be friends.'

'You wouldn't let it be awkward because you're a total professional and you put your patients first,' Rob said. 'And there's also no reason why it should go wrong. And, as you said, it's temporary—so why not let yourself be happy while you're here?'

'It's too soon.'

'It's nearly four months. To me, you're on the verge of wallowing—and I can be that harsh because you're my brother and I love you too much to let you carry on being miserable.' Rob shook his head. 'Tabby really hurt you, I know, but the best way to get over a break-up is to meet someone else.'

'That's cynical, Rob.'

'It's a fact, little brother,' Rob said lightly. 'Maybe your nurse practitioner would be good for you.'

'I'm not a user, Rob.'

Rob frowned, 'Of course you're not. What I'm trying to say, in my very clumsy way, is that you've had a rough few months. And you're here for the next three months. Spending a little time with someone you like, getting to know each other and having a bit of fun—it might help you move on. Don't let what happened with Tabby put you off dating anyone else.'

'You're not dating anyone, either,' Ollie pointed out.

'Because I'm still recovering from major surgery.'

Ollie just looked at his brother.

'All right. I like the thrill of the chase and I haven't met anyone who's made me want to settle down. Even though we're practically identical, I'm wired differently from you, Ollie. You can settle. I have itchy feet. And I admit, I get bored easily.' Rob sighed. 'Perhaps it's true about there being a good twin and a bad twin. You're the good one.'

'You're not the "bad twin" at all, Rob. We just want different things.'

'I'm sorry that I caused your break-up with Tabby...'

'You didn't cause the break-up,' Ollie said.

'Look at it logically. It was my fault. If my kidneys hadn't failed, you wouldn't have suggested moving your wedding day and it wouldn't have escalated into—well, cancelling it. Though I still think the reason she gave you for calling it off was seriously weak.'

'She grew up seeing her mum put her life on hold for her dad, and she didn't want that kind of future for herself. I can understand that,' Ollie said, 'even if I don't think I would've given her that kind of future.'

'Maybe you had a lucky escape,' Rob said. 'Because if the going got tough she wouldn't have stuck it out.'

Or maybe he just wasn't *enough* for anyone, Ollie thought.

'You've got your brooding face on. Stop,' Rob said.

'Sorry. I really thought she was the right one. Which makes me pretty hopeless at judging people,' Ollie said.

Rob clapped his shoulder. 'Actually, it

makes you human. Everyone makes mistakes. Just don't close yourself off.'

'Be more Rob, and take a risk?' Ollie asked wryly.

'Just as I'm going to try to be more Ollie, and be sensible,' Rob said. 'So, between us, we can be the best we can be. Deal?'

Ollie thought about it. Be more like his twin. Take risks. The idea put him into a cold sweat; over the years, Rob had taken more than enough risks for both of them.

'Olls,' Rob said softly. 'It'll do both of us good.'

Put like that, how could he refuse? 'Deal.'

On Friday morning, Ollie arrived at the surgery to discover a tray of individually wrapped brownies, lemon cake and oatmeal cookies on one of the low tables, with a plastic jar labelled 'Donations' beside them and a folded card announcing 'Gemma's Friday Fundraisers are back!'

Clearly this was what his colleague had spent her day off doing. Baking.

There was another card on the tray, listing the ingredients in each recipe with the potential allergens highlighted in bold.

Smiling, he picked up a cookie and some

lemon cake, and dropped some money into her box.

'What's this—buying cake?' Gemma teased, walking into the reception area. 'I thought you weren't a cake person?'

'I'm not. I'm buying this for my next-door neighbours,' he said. 'I thought they might like a Friday treat.'

'That's kind of you.'

'They've kept an eye out for me since I moved in. It's the least I can do,' he said.

'Are you still OK for the quiz team tonight?' she asked.

'Yes.'

'Good. See you there. Triage awaits,' she said with a smile.

Midway through the morning, Ollie was just writing up his notes when Maddie, the receptionist, burst into his room. 'Dr Langley, help! One of our patients has just collapsed in the waiting room.'

'I'm coming,' Ollie said, grabbing his stethoscope. 'Did you see what happened?'

'No. I was helping a patient when someone else in the waiting room screamed and I saw Mrs Henderson on the floor. Apparently she just fell off her chair.'

There were three main causes of collapse:

fainting, seizures and heart problems. Given that Maddie hadn't mentioned Mrs Henderson's shaking limbs, it was likely to be fainting or a cardiac issue. 'Get the defibrillator,' he said, 'find out if anyone saw her hit her head, and I might need you to call an ambulance—and manage the patients in the waiting room, please, so we can give her a bit of privacy.'

'Got it,' Maddie said.

The middle-aged woman was still lying on the floor when they went into the reception area.

'Can you hear me, Mrs Henderson?' Ollie asked loudly, shaking her shoulder as he knelt beside her.

There was no response.

He tilted her head back to clear her airway.

'I've got the defib and she didn't hit her head,' Gemma said, joining him. 'The patient next to her said she just collapsed.'

'Do you by any chance know her medical history?'

'Yes. Nicole Henderson has high blood pressure—she's actually due for a check with me, this morning, because the last two medications I've tried with her haven't worked, and she had a bad reaction to beta blockers.'

This was sounding more and more like a

cardiac event. 'Her airway's clear but she's not breathing,' he said. 'I'll start CPR. Can you turn the defib—'

'Already done,' she cut in. 'I'll do the sticky pads. Maddie's got everyone outside so we're good to go. I'll call the ambulance, too.'

She placed the pads on each side of Mrs Henderson's chest. He stopped doing CPR so the machine could analyse Mrs Henderson's heart rhythm. The recorded voice on the defibrillator informed them it was administering a shock, then told him, when it had no effect, to continue CPR.

Gemma had got through to the emergency services. 'The ambulance is on its way,' she said.

Between them, they kept going with chest compressions and breathing, stopping only when the defibrillator's recorded voice told them it needed to check the patient's heart rhythm.

By the time the paramedics arrived and loaded her into the ambulance, Nicole Henderson still hadn't regained consciousness.

'This isn't looking great,' Ollie said wearily. 'Poor woman. Hopefully they'll get her heart restarted on the way in to hospital.'

They both knew that the longer it took to restart the heart, the worse the prognosis. And, given that Gemma's sister had died from a heart condition, Ollie knew this must be tough for her. 'Are you OK?' he asked.

She nodded. 'I just feel I've let my patient down.'

'You couldn't have predicted this,' he said. 'And we did our best here. In some ways, this is the best place she could've collapsed, because we have a defib and enough knowledge between us to give her the right help.'

'I know. It's just…' She grimaced.

He reached out and squeezed her hand. 'You had the defib switched on and the pads ready almost before I could ask. Nobody could've done more. And she might be fine.'

Except the hospital called later that afternoon to say that Nicole Henderson hadn't made it.

He typed Got a minute? on the practice messaging system and sent it to Gemma.

Yes.

Ollie made her a mug of coffee and rapped on her door. 'Sorry, it's not good news. She didn't make it.'

Gemma sighed. 'Poor woman. She was the head of the local junior school. She wasn't popular—let's just say her predecessor was very different and everyone was upset when she retired, because she always fought for the kids and she was great with the parents and teachers—but even so I don't think anyone would actually wish her dead.'

'Don't blame yourself,' he said. 'I reviewed her notes when I wrote up what happened, and I would've treated her the way you did.'

'If only she hadn't rescheduled her appointment from last week.'

'It might still have happened, and it might've been somewhere that didn't have a defib.'

'I suppose so. Thank you for being kind.' She took a deep breath. 'I have referrals to write up and I'm guessing you have paperwork, too. So I won't hold you up. But I appreciate the coffee.'

'You're welcome.' He paused. 'I don't mean this to sound as tactless as it does, but will the quiz tonight be cancelled?'

She shook her head. 'I think, if anything, we need a reminder that there's a bright side to life. And that's not meant to sound callous.'

Gemma Baxter wasn't anything remotely approaching callous, he thought. 'OK. I'll see you later.'

The pub where Ollie had arranged to meet Gemma and the team was only a few minutes' walk from his cottage; when he arrived, the rest of his team was already there, and Gemma stood up to wave to him.

He hadn't seen her out of her uniform before; her faded jeans hugged her curves, and her hair was loose rather than tied back as she wore it for work. Yet again, he was struck by how pretty she was, and it almost made him tongue-tied. Which was crazy. He wasn't looking to get involved with anyone. Yet his twin's words echoed in his head.

'Spending a little time with someone you like, getting to know each other and having a bit of fun—it might help you move on.'

He made his way over to their table.

'Time for introductions,' Gemma said. 'Everyone, this is Oliver—he's Aadya's locum for the next three months.' She swiftly introduced him to the people round the table he hadn't yet met.

'Hello, everyone.' He smiled. 'Can I get anyone a drink?'

'No, we're all sorted,' Kyle, one of the other practice doctors, said, smiling back. 'I heard about Nicole Henderson. You've had a bit of a rough start to your time with us.'

'I'm just sorry I couldn't do more,' Ollie said. 'I hope it's not going to worry Aadya

Devi's patients, the idea of having to see me when I've already lost a patient.'

'You and Gemma did everything you could,' Kyle said. 'Nobody's going to blame you.'

Ollie nodded his thanks. But the time he'd sorted out a pint and ordered his food, he was chatting with the others as if he'd always known them.

The quiz turned out to be great fun; although he was woefully inadequate on the local history round, he managed to get a couple of the musical intros that the others couldn't remember, as well as a really obscure geography question.

'How on earth did you know that?' Maddie asked.

'My twin's a climber,' Ollie said. 'He's the adventurous one; I'm the one with common sense.'

'There's nothing wrong with having two feet on the ground,' Kyle said. 'As I would dearly love to tell every single holidaymaker here who tries one of the water activities for the first time and tries to keep up with people who do it all the time, and ends up with a sprain or a strains or a fracture,' he added ruefully.

'Rob—my twin—got a bit excited about

the idea of kite-surfing,' Oliver said. 'But he's having to be more me at the moment. He's recovering from a kidney transplant.'

'Ouch. That sounds nasty,' Fayola, their midwife, said. 'What happened?'

'Burst appendix followed by blood poisoning, and it wiped out his kidneys. He was helping with the aftermath of an earthquake at the time,' Ollie explained.

'Oh, now that's unfair,' Lakshmi, their pharmacist, said, sounding sympathetic. 'Poor guy.'

'He's doing well now,' Ollie said. 'But that's why I moved up here from London for a while, to support him and our parents.'

He caught Gemma's raised eyebrow; but he wasn't comfortable putting himself in the role of hero. Anyone would've done the same, in his shoes. Nobody else needed to know that he'd been the living kidney donor.

In the end, their team came second.

'And if anyone hasn't sponsored our Gemma for the skydive,' the quizmaster said, 'come and see us at the bar, because we've got a sponsorship form right here. And there's a collecting tin if you've got any spare change.'

Ollie really liked the fact that the whole village seemed to be so supportive of Gemma's efforts. It felt good to be part of a community like this. In London, he'd found that people kept themselves to themselves a lot more.

They stayed on for another drink after the quiz was over, and then the others all had to be back for their babysitters. Ollie looked at Gemma. 'Do you need to be anywhere right now?'

'No. Why?'

'I was going for a walk on the beach, to see the first stars coming out—something I couldn't really do in London. Do you want to join me?'

'That'd be nice,' she said.

They walked down to the beach together. The sea looked almost navy in the late summer evening light, and the first stars were peeking through. The moon was low and shone a silvery path across the sea. The waves were swishing gently across the shore, the rhythm soft and almost hypnotic, and Ollie felt the day's tensions starting to melt.

'That's the thing about living by the sea. If the day's been tough you can go for a walk and let the swoosh of the water wash the misery away,' she said.

'There were good bits to the day, too,' he said. 'But, yeah, losing a patient in my first week here is a bit of a shaky start.'

'It wasn't your fault,' she said. 'If it's anyone's fault, it's mine, but you argued me out of that earlier. We did our best, and that's all anyone can ask.'

'I guess.'

She stopped. 'Oliver.'

He stopped, too, and turned to face her. 'What?'

'Right now,' she said, 'I think you need a hug.' To his surprise, she took a step towards him and wrapped her arms round him.

Being this close to her meant he could smell the floral scent of her perfume. Light, sweet and summery, it made him think of sunshine. Being hugged by her was like being bathed in sunshine, too, and he couldn't resist wrapping his arms round her.

The waves swished onto the shore, and all Ollie was aware of was the beating of her heart, in the same strong, fierce rhythm as his own. The connection was irresistible, and he found his face pressed against hers. And then it was, oh, so easy to tilt his face just a fraction more, so the corner of his mouth was brushing against hers. His mouth tingled, and he couldn't help holding her closer, moving his face just a fraction further so he was really kissing her, and she was kissing him back.

His head was spinning and it felt as if fireworks were going off overhead, bright star-bursts. Even though he knew he shouldn't be doing this—it was too soon after Tabby, and Gemma was his new colleague and he didn't want to complicate things—he couldn't help himself. This felt so *right*. Kissing Gemma, the sea singing a lullaby in the background, her arms wrapped as tightly round him as his were round her...

The moment seemed to last for ever, a moment of sweetness that was like balm to his aching heart.

And then it ended, and he found himself taking a step back and staring at Gemma.

'I'm sorry,' he said. 'That wasn't meant to happen.' A momentary—and major—lapse of reason.

'I think we've both had a tough day and we got caught up in the moonlight,' Gemma said. 'Let's pretend it didn't happen.'

The problem was, Ollie knew he'd rather like it to happen again. But she clearly didn't, so he'd have to ignore his feelings. 'OK. Can I at least walk you home? I know you're local and you're perfectly capable of looking after yourself, but it's dark and...well, it's the way I was brought up.'

'Gallant. I like that.'

And there was no edge to her tone, no

mockery; Ollie had the strongest feeling that Gemma understood him and appreciated him.

They walked back to her flat in a companionable silence. At the entrance to the flats, she said, 'Would you like to come in for coffee?'

Part of him did; yet, at the same time, he knew it wasn't a good idea. He could still remember the touch of her mouth against his and the scent of her hair; it would be more sensible to put a little distance between them so he could get his common sense back. 'Maybe another time?'

She nodded. 'Sure. Goodnight, Oliver.'

'Goodnight, Gemma. See you at work on Monday.'

Ollie spent Sunday with his family, as planned; and the influx of summer visitors and extra people needing medical help meant that he didn't actually have a proper lunch break until Wednesday. He'd just stepped into the bakery when he realised that Gemma was there.

'Great minds think alike,' he said with a smile. 'Are you heading up to the cliffs?'

'I certainly am,' she said. 'You're welcome to join me.'

'Thanks. I'd like that.'

Once they were settled on her picnic blanket, he said, 'So do you have much planned for the week?'

'I'm babysitting my goddaughter Scarlett—Claire's three-year-old—on Friday night, so she and Andy can have a proper date night. Which means I get Claire's amazing macaroni cheese for dinner; then Scarlett and I will sing our way through all the songs from *The Little Mermaid* during her bath; and then I get cuddles and tell her stories until she falls asleep.'

She grinned. 'And then I have a hot date with a classic rom-com, a mug of tea, and some of Claire's ginger cake. Friday night doesn't get better than this.'

His idea of a perfect Friday night sounded a lot like Gemma's. Cuddling up on the sofa with a good film, winding down after a busy week…

'How about you?' she asked.

'Nothing in particular,' he said. 'I might go for a walk on the beach on Saturday. Didn't you say something about a shipwreck being visible?'

'There is, at low tide.' She took her phone from her bag and looked something up. 'Low tide is at four o'clock on Saturday afternoon. If you don't mind a friend tagging along, maybe I could join you for that walk and tell you all the touristy stuff about the wreck.'

'I'd like that,' he said. 'And maybe we can grab fish and chips afterwards, and eat it sitting on the harbour wall.'

'Great idea,' she said with a smile. 'I haven't had fish and chips for ages. Which is a terrible admission, given that we live in a seaside village.'

Funny how her smile made him feel so warm inside. 'Fish and chips is mandatory,' he said, smiling back. 'I like mine with lots of salt and vinegar, but shhh, don't tell our patients that because I nag everyone about their salt intake…'

She laughed. 'Me, too. For both!'

Gemma spent most of Thursday cleaning her flat and baking for her charity cake stall; on Friday, she didn't see Oliver more than once in passing, though he did text her at lunchtime to check that she was still available for their walk on Saturday afternoon.

On Friday afternoon, Mrs Brown, the history teacher she remembered from school, came in. 'I'm so sorry, wasting your time coming in with something as minor as a rash,' she said. 'I did go to the pharmacy on Monday, but the hydrocortisone cream they gave me hasn't helped. The rash is spreading.' She grimaced. 'The itchiness is *unbelievable*. And it's keeping me awake at night.'

'Let me have a look, Mrs Brown,' Gemma said.

Mrs Brown rolled up her cotton trousers to her knees, and Gemma examined the rash. There were pinpricks of deep red on the edges, and the middle sections were raised with a flat surface.

'It looks like an allergic reaction, so we'll start with the obvious stuff. Have you made any changes to your detergents or toiletries over the last couple of weeks?'

'No, and it's not a change in formulation because they're the same batch I've used for a couple of weeks. I'm paranoid about ticks since Harvey—my spaniel—got one last year, so I always wear long trousers on dog-walks, and I haven't brushed against any plants or knelt on anything with bare legs.' Mrs Brown shook her head, seeming puzzled. 'I haven't eaten anything out of the usual, and my blood-pressure tablets are the same ones I've been on for years and years.'

'So that rules out all the usual suspects,' Gemma said.

Mrs Brown grimaced. 'I did wonder if

it was shingles—I've heard that's horribly itchy.'

'Usually a shingles rash is only on one side of the body and doesn't cross the midline. This is on both shins, so I'm pretty sure it's not that,' Gemma said. 'Have you ever had eczema or psoriasis?'

'No, and the only things I'm allergic to are penicillin and fabric plasters—neither of which I've been in contact with for years.'

'OK. It's possible to develop allergies at any time of life,' Gemma said, 'so what I'm going to prescribe is something generic that should help. Colloidal oats to wash with, an emollient to keep your legs moisturised, a slightly stronger steroid cream to use twice a day to try and calm the rash down, and an antihistamine which should stop the itching. Until that kicks in, cold compresses are your best friend. And obviously you're sensible enough to know not to scratch.'

'So you've no idea what's causing it?'

'There are about three thousand different rashes,' Gemma said with a smile, 'so, at the moment, all I can say is it's a red, itchy rash and we don't currently know the cause. Or, if you want it in medical-speak, it's erythematous idiopathic pruritic macules.'

'Which sounds a bit more impressive,' Mrs Brown said with a wry smile.

'If it doesn't improve in the next three or four days, come back and I'll do a swab test and refer you to the dermatologist.' Gemma printed out the prescriptions and handed them over. 'Cold compresses will definitely help to stop the itching.'

She changed at work and went straight to Claire's, where she enjoyed a catch-up with her best friend before Claire and Andy went out for the evening.

Spending time with Scarlett was always fun. They drew pictures and played games until dinner, and then it was bath time.

'Just one more, Aunty Gemma!' Scarlett pleaded.

'Nope. We've done *all* the songs,' Gemma said, and lifted her goddaughter from the bath to wrap her in a towel. 'Time to dry off before you get all wrinkly. And then it's a glass of milk, brush your teeth, and a story.'

'Two stories? Please, please, *please*?' Scarlett wheedled.

Gemma laughed. 'All right. Two stories. Let's get you dry and put your PJs on.'

Given the disaster of her love life—since she'd graduated, all her relationships had

ended really quickly—Gemma thought that
her goddaughter was probably the nearest
she'd ever get to having a little one of her
own. And she knew she was lucky. Some people didn't even have that.

After she'd settled Scarlett to sleep, she
made herself a mug of tea and switched on
the film. It was one of her favourites, and
she must have seen it a dozen times over the
years, but it still made her smile.

Apart from one thing.

The main actor's colouring was exactly the
same as Oliver's. And Oliver's smile—rare,
but genuine—made her heart beat just as fast
as the actor's did.

She really was going to have to be sensible
tomorrow. Even though there was something
about him that made her want to forget all
about caution. Or maybe especially because
he tempted her to stop being careful and take
a risk, she corrected herself. He was only here
temporarily. The most they could offer each
other was a summer of fun. Which might be
a good thing: but Gemma was scared that
if she let him close then she'd start to want
more. And what if he didn't want the same?
What if he left after three months and didn't
ask her to go with him?

So it would be better to stick to being

friends. Forget that kiss and the way his had made her blood feel as if it was fizzing through her veins.

Oliver Langley was her colleague.

Full stop.

CHAPTER FIVE

SATURDAY WAS BRIGHT and sunny, and Gemma met Oliver at the harbour.

'Time for your touristy trip,' she said. 'We'll start with the spooky local legend, see the seals, then see the shipwreck,' she said with a smile.

'Bring it on,' Oliver said, smiling back. 'What's the spooky bit? A grey lady or something?'

'No, it's a barghest.'

'I've never heard of that,' he said.

'It's a huge black dog with massive teeth and claws and fiery eyes, which only comes out at night. Apparently if you see him, it's a portent of doom. It's left up to your imagination what that doom might be.' She laughed. 'It's very similar to the "black dog" story told all over the country, though. My theory is that the legend was started by smugglers, who hung lanterns with red covers round their ponies' necks to make it look like fiery eyes. If people were scared of the legend of the giant black dog, it meant they'd stay away from the cliffs—and that would mean they were less likely to discover the smugglers' tunnels and any contraband.'

'So there were smugglers at Ashermouth Bay?' he asked.

'There were in most places along the coast in the eighteenth century,' she said. 'There are tunnels in the cliff which lead to the Manor House and the rectory. They used to smuggle brandy, gin and tea. I remember doing the *Watch the Wall, My Darling* at school, and our teacher told us all about the tunnels. Most of the older houses in the village have little hiding places.'

'That's fascinating,' he said. 'Can you actually go down the tunnels now?'

'Strictly guided tours only, and it depends on the tide,' she said. 'The teacher who told us about the tunnels also said that she went in them when she was our age, with some friends; they had to be rescued by the lifeboat team, and one of her friends nearly drowned. And then she casually mentioned that there are rats everywhere, and huge spiders.'

'Enough to put you all off the idea of being brave and exploring by yourself?'

'Indeed.'

Gemma enjoyed walking with Oliver along the damp sand. A couple of times, his hand accidentally brushed hers and sent a zing of awareness through her skin; yet again, she remembered the way he'd kissed her on the beach a week ago, and it made her knees weak. Not wanting to be needy, she took refuge in the guided tour she was supposed to be giving him. 'Next, we have the seals,' she said. 'There's a big colony of grey seals, a bit further up the coast, but these ones are common seals. Their pups are born in June and July, and everyone comes to see them in the bay.'

Oliver looked entranced by the seals, the babies with their white fur and their parents undulating their way slowly along the sand, while others ducked and dived in the water.

'That's lovely. I can see why people come here,' he said.

They'd just reached the roped-off area when they saw a small boy running on the sand. A woman ducked under the rope—his mother, Gemma guessed—but before she could reach him he fell over, next to one of the seal pups. An older seal lunged at him, and he screamed.

'Jake!' the woman called, and sped over to grab him.

'Hopefully the seal just scared him, rather than bit him,' Gemma said.

But the little boy appeared to be clutching at his hand and crying.

'Can we help?' Oliver asked as the woman, carrying the child, ducked back under the rope next to them. 'I'm a doctor—my name's Oliver—and Gemma here's a nurse practitioner.'

'The seal bit him,' the woman said. 'I told Jake not to go near them. I *told* him we had to look at them from afar, but he ran off and went into the roped-off area before I could stop him.'

'We saw him fall,' Gemma said.

'I know seals are protective of their pups at this time of year—that's why the ropes are there—but I…' She shook her head, looking anguished.

'Let's get you over to the lifeguards' hut. They'll have a first-aid kit,' Oliver said.

Between them, they ushered Jake and his mother to the lifeguards' hut.

'Hey, Gem. What's happened?' the lifeguard asked.

'Hi, Callum.' Gemma explained swiftly and introduced Oliver.

'Could we have some hot water, some antiseptic and a dressing?' Oliver asked.

'Sure. I'll fetch them,' Callum said.

Gemma crouched down by the little boy, who was still crying. 'Jake, will you let me look at your hand?'

He shook his head, guarding his hand, and her heart sank.

'Jake, do you want to see a magic trick?' Oliver asked.

It was the last thing she'd expected but, to her relief, the distraction worked, and the little boy nodded.

'See how my hands are open?' Oliver asked, waggling his fingers. 'I need you to put your hands exactly like that, making a star shape with your fingers—but I want you to hold them *really* still—and then I want you to guess the magic word.'

Genius, Gemma thought as the little boy opened both his hands, the shock and pain of the bite forgotten.

'Please!' Jake said.

She couldn't help smiling. 'That's a good magic word.'

'But not the one I'm looking for,' Oliver said. 'Try again.'

Gemma examined Jake's hand while Oliver encouraged the little boy to guess more magic words.

To her relief, the bite was shallow, more

of a graze than anything else; but she also knew that a seal's mouth could contain bacteria that could cause a very nasty complication, and the little boy would need a course of antibiotics.

'It's going to sting a bit,' Gemma warned when Callum brought the hot water and antiseptic over. 'Unfortunately our surgery's closed until Monday morning or I'd say call in and we'd prescribe antibiotics.'

'Antibiotics?' Jake's mum looked shocked.

'Are you local or on holiday?' Gemma asked.

'On holiday from Birmingham—this is our first day.'

'Then you need to go either to the walk-in centre in the next town, or to the emergency department at the hospital,' Gemma said. 'Take a seal letter with you, and they'll sort out some tetracycline to make sure an infection doesn't start.'

'Seal letter?' Oliver asked.

'Tetracycline's the most effective antibiotic against the Mycoplasma organism in a seal's mouth,' Gemma explained. 'It's why we have a seal letter for people to take to whatever medical department they go to. If a seal bite isn't treated properly, and the wrong antibiotic is given, the person could develop a complication called "seal finger".'

'Abracadabra!' Jake shouted.

'That's the right magic word. And look what I've found behind your ear,' Oliver said, plucking a coin from behind Jake's ear.

The little boy's eyes were round with amazement. 'That's real magic!'

'It certainly is,' Oliver said with a smile. 'Jake, I'm going to need to wash your hands with some very special soap and water.'

Callum had got a bowl of warm water ready, along with antiseptic soap, and Gemma encouraged Jake to wash his hands.

It obviously stung and the little boy pulled his hands out of the water and cried, but then Oliver stepped in again.

'I'll wash my hands with you,' he said. 'And we'll sing a special washing hands song. Do you know "If You're Happy and You Know it?"'

Jake nodded.

'We're going to change the words a bit,' Oliver said, taking his watch off and stuffing it into the pocket of his jeans. 'Instead of "clap your hands", we'll sing "wash your hands". Ready? And we'll get your mummy to sing it, too.'

'Yay!' Jake said, the stinging forgotten.

Oliver got them to sing along. It didn't matter that his voice was flat; he was so good with the little boy that it put a lump in her throat.

When Jake's hands were clean, Oliver gently helped dry them.

The wound was still bleeding a little bit— to Gemma's relief, because it meant she didn't have to hurt Jake by squeezing the wound to make it bleed. She put a pad over it and a dressing.

'Here's the seal letter,' Callum said, handing it to Jake's mum. 'And I've written the phone number and address of the walk-in centre and the hospital's emergency department on the back for you.'

'Thank you. I'll take him now,' Jake's mum said. 'And thank you, both of you, for helping.'

'That's what we're here for,' Oliver said with a smile.

Once Jake and his mum had left, Callum said, 'Thanks for the back-up, guys. Really appreciated.'

'No worries. Give my love to Sadie when you see her next,' Gemma said, and shepherded Oliver out of the lifeguards' hut. 'Sadie's his big sister. She was one of my sister's best friends,' she explained.

'I'm guessing everyone knows everyone in Ashermouth Bay?' Oliver asked.

'Pretty much,' she said with a smile.

'I have to say, I've never heard of "seal finger" before,' he said.

'To be fair, it's probably not that common in London,' she said.

'But it happens a lot here?'

'There have been a few cases, over the years. I didn't like to say, in front of Jake's mum, but it involves inflammation and cellulitis, and it used to mean the finger would have to be amputated.'

'That's pretty major stuff. So how do you know all about seals?'

'I was a seal warden, the summers when I was fifteen and sixteen. It meant I did a two-hour shift on the beach, most days, talking to visitors about the seals, answering their questions, advising them where to get the best views of the seals and also making sure they stayed well clear of the roped-off area where the seals were resting. If you get too close to the pups, you could scare the mum away and there's a risk she'll abandon the baby.'

'A seal warden.' He raised an eyebrow. 'You're full of surprises.'

'I wanted to be a vet, when I was fifteen,' she said. 'Though, after Sarah died, I decided

I wanted to help people rather than animals, so I trained to be a nurse instead.'

'You're good with people,' he said. 'So do you have pets?'

'No. I work full-time, it's just me at home and I live in a flat, so it wouldn't be fair to have a dog. But I do walk a couple of dogs down my road, sometimes.' She looked at him. 'I assume you don't have pets, either?'

'No, and for the same reason. It really wouldn't be fair in London.'

Which reminded her. He was here temporarily. 'Do you think you'll go back to London?'

'I'll see how things go with Rob,' he said. 'Probably.'

And it was ridiculous that her stomach swooped in disappointment.

She kept the conversation light, telling him more about the seals and pointing out the shipwreck. They climbed up the path to the castle on the other side of the bay, then walked back along the cliffs and back down to the harbour. Every so often, his hand brushed against hers, and it felt like electricity zinging along her skin.

What if his fingers caught hers?

What if he held her hand?

It made her feel like a teenager again, waiting for the boy she had a crush on to notice her.

But Oliver had clearly had second thoughts since their kiss on the beach, and he was exquisitely polite with her. Gemma was cross with herself for being disappointed; hadn't she learned the hard way not to rely on other people for her happiness? So she pasted a bright, sparkling smile on her face and pretended everything was just fine.

When they reached the harbour and stood in the queue for the fish and chips, Ollie said, 'This is my shout, by the way.'

'We'll go halves,' Gemma countered.

He shook his head. 'You were kind enough to show me round. It's the least I can do.'

She smiled. 'All right. Thank you.'

They sat on the harbour wall, eating their fish and chips from the recyclable boxes, watching the boats and the gentle swish of the sea. How much slower life was here than it was in London, Ollie thought. And he was really beginning to enjoy living by the sea.

After they'd eaten, he walked her home. A couple of times, his hand brushed against hers, and he was so tempted to hold her hand. But that wasn't the deal they'd agreed. They were friends; and he still didn't trust his judgement. He didn't want to rush this.

They came to a halt outside a small block of flats.

'Would you like to come in for coffee?' she asked.

Ollie knew he ought to make an excuse, but he was curious to know what Gemma's inner sanctum was like. 'That'd be nice,' he said.

'I'm on the ground floor,' she said, and let them into the lobby before unlocking her front door. 'The bathroom's here on the left.'

She said nothing about the closed door on the right, which he assumed was her bedroom.

'Living room,' she said as they walked into the next room. 'And my kitchen-diner's through there. You take your coffee without milk, don't you?'

'And no sugar. Yes, please,' he said.

'Take a seat, and I'll bring the coffee through.'

The whole room was neat and tidy. The walls were neutral, as were the comfortable sofa and armchair with a reading lamp, but there was a throw the colour of sunshine across the back of the sofa, and the material of the cushions was covered in sunflowers. On the mantelpiece there was a vase of sunflowers—clearly Gemma's favourite flowers.

There were framed photographs surrounding the vase; one was of Gemma herself, and a younger girl who looked so much like her that Ollie guessed it was Sarah. There was another of Gemma holding a baby, which he guessed would be the goddaughter she'd mentioned earlier in the week, plus one of her with her fellow students at graduation. There was a photo of Gemma in a bridesmaid's dress, laughing with the bride; he vaguely recognised the other woman, and guessed that was Claire.

There were no photos, he noticed, of Gemma with her parents. Given how family-oriented Gemma seemed, that surprised him.

On the wall was a framed pen-and-ink drawing of seals on the beach.

'That's an amazing picture,' he said when she came back in, carrying two mugs of coffee.

'Sarah drew me that for my sixteenth birthday. It still amazes me to think she was only twelve at the time.'

'She was very talented,' Ollie said, meaning it.

Tears shimmered for a moment in Gemma's dark eyes. 'I loved her so much. But I know she'd be furious with me if I moped around—just as I would've been furious with her if I'd been the one who'd died and she'd been left behind to deal with it.'

If Rob had died from that burst appendix, Ollie thought, he wasn't sure he would've coped well with it. And he was thirty, not a teenager.

'I think she'd be really proud of you,' he said. 'You don't mope at all. Look at what you've achieved. You're a nurse practitioner, and you make a difference to people's lives every single working day. Plus you've raised a lot of money for the cardiac centre where she was treated.'

His kindness was nearly Gemma's undoing. 'I hope she'd be proud of me,' she said.

'What's not to be proud of? If you were my sister, I'd be boasting about you,' he said.

Sisterly wasn't quite the way she was feeling about him, but she damped that down. If he'd wanted to take things further between them, he would've taken her hand on the beach or said something.

'Thank you,' she said instead.

'So you're a reader?' He gestured to her bookcase.

'I love historicals,' she said. 'Yvonne—Claire's mum—got me reading historical crime when I was in sixth form, to give me a break from studying. I loved *The Cadfael Chronicles* series. And then I discovered historical romance.' She paused. 'So are you a reader?'

'Not as much as my mum would like,' he said with a smile. 'I tend to read non-fiction. Journals and the like. And I have a bad habit of watching documentaries.'

'Nothing wrong with that,' she said. 'Though I love films. Musicals and comedies, mainly.'

'With a bit of skydiving on the side.' He smiled. 'The sort of thing my twin would do.'

'I'm really not that brave,' she said. 'The skydiving's a one-off. Though I'm doing a sixty-mile cycle ride down the coast, next month.' She gave him a sidelong look. 'Are you a cyclist?'

'No. But I'll sponsor you,' he said.

'I wasn't dropping a hint.'

'I know, but it's important to you. And I'm your friend, so I'll support you.'

Friend.

Oliver had just made it very clear how he saw her.

So she'd just have to stop secretly wishing for more.

It was another busy week; and Mrs Brown called Gemma on Tuesday. 'I've been taking photographs of the rash, just so you can see how it's changed.'

Gemma looked at the photographs. 'It's definitely looking angrier. It's spreading, and the spots are coalescing.'

'And it's so, so *itchy*. It's keeping me awake at night.'

'Can you email the pictures to me, please?' She gave Mrs Brown the surgery's email address. 'I'm going to have a word with one of my colleagues,' she said, 'and I'll call you back.'

When the photographs arrived, she sent over a note through the practice messaging system.

How are you with rashes? Could do with another pair of eyes.

Oliver called her. 'Is your patient with you right now?'

'No. She's just sent me some photographs. I've added them to her notes.' She gave Oliver the details.

'Let's have a look.' He paused, and she guessed he was checking the file on his screen. 'Actually, you've treated it as I would've done. If it's not responding to steroid cream, I'd say ask her to do a swab test, to see if there's bacterial or viral involvement.'

'And if it's not that, then a referral to Dermatology?'

'Good call,' he said.

Gemma rang Mrs Brown and asked her to drop into the surgery later that morning to do a swab test, then called her next patient.

Eileen Townsend was eighty-one, diabetic, and her daughter had brought her in because she was having a lot of falls. Gemma knew that diabetes could cause elderly patients to have more falls than non-diabetics, because hypoglycaemia could cause light-headedness. She always worried about her elderly patients having a fall, with the extra risk of breaking bones; and reduced mobility often went hand in hand with foot care problems, which a diabetic might not notice.

'I help Mum with her medication,' Mrs Townsend's daughter said, 'and she had her six-monthly check with you three months ago.'

Gemma nodded. 'Nothing's changed since then?'

'Not really,' Mrs Townsend said.

Gemma double-checked her notes. There had been no hospital admissions and no suggestion that Mrs Townsend had had a stroke or developed Parkinson's. Maybe postural hypotension? 'Are you feeling light-headed at all before you fall, Mrs Townsend?'

'No. It just happens,' Mrs Townsend said.

'Would you mind me assessing you physically?' she asked.

'No. Just tell me what I need to do.'

'Can you stand up for me, please?'

Mrs Townsend stood up, and Gemma was pleased to see that she didn't sway, raise her arms or move her feet to balance.

'Wonderful. Can you lift one foot off the floor, just a little bit?'

She struggled to balance on her right foot, and Gemma made a note.

'Lovely. Can you walk round the room for me?' Gemma chatted to her as she walked, and was pleased to see that Mrs Townsend didn't stop walking when she answered a question.

'That's great. And, lastly, I'd like to try one more thing. I'd like you to sit down, walk over to the window, turn round, walk back to the chair and sit down again.'

Gemma timed her, and was pleased to note that it took less than twelve seconds.

'That's all really good,' she said. 'The only thing I think you're struggling with is balance. There are some good strength and balance exercises you can do using a chair—I can print some off for you.' She smiled at Mrs Townsend's daughter. 'And if you can help your mum do the exercises, that'd be brilliant. Though I'd like to try and set up some classes locally. I'll run that one by the head of the practice, and if I can make it happen I'll let you know.'

'Of course I can help my mum,' Mrs Townsend's daughter said.

'Brilliant. The other thing I'd like to do is send the occupational health team out to you for a hazards assessment of your home.'

'I've already checked the hazards. There aren't any trailing wires, I make Mum wear slippers with proper soles so she doesn't slip on the floor, and there aren't any rugs she can trip over,' Mrs Townsend's daughter said.

'That's excellent,' Gemma said. 'But it's not just about hazards you can see—it's looking at how you use the space and what they can do to help. So they might suggest putting risers on the bottom of an armchair to make it easier for your mum to stand up, or a grab rail next to a toilet or a bath. Plus they can set you up with an alarm you wear round your neck, Mrs Townsend, so you can get help really quickly if you do have a fall.'

'I don't want to wear something round my

neck,' Mrs Townsend said. 'I'm old, not useless.'

'Of course you're not useless,' Gemma said. 'But you've had a few falls, and your daughter's worried about you—just as I'd be worried if my mum had a few falls. I'd be panicking that she'd fall at night and nobody would know—so she'd just have to lie there in the cold, unable to get up again until someone came in the next morning.'

Mrs Townsend's daughter nodded. 'That's my biggest fear. Mum, if you wore something round your neck so I knew you could get help when you needed it, that'd stop me panicking so much.'

'I suppose you're right,' Mrs Townsend said with a sigh. 'I don't want to lose my independence.'

'An alarm would actually give you a bit more independence because it'd stop your daughter worrying so much,' Gemma said gently.

'All right. I'll do it,' Mrs Townsend agreed.

'I'll sort out the referral,' Gemma promised, 'and they'll call you in a few days to organise a visit.' She printed off the exercises. 'These will all help with your balance and core strength, which means you're less likely to fall.'

'Ballet's meant to be good for that,' her daughter said.

'I'm too old to start being a ballerina,' Mrs Townsend said. 'I can't do all that leaping about.'

'Actually, there are special classes for older beginners,' Gemma said. 'My best friend's mum does it. And not only is it good for her balance, it's also meant she's made new friends. She says it's the best thing she's ever done. I can get the details from her, if you like.'

'That would be really good,' her daughter said. She smiled. 'Your social life will be better than mine, at this rate, Mum.'

'All right. I'll give it a go,' Mrs Townsend said.

Once her patient had gone, Gemma sent a note to Oliver over the practice internal email.

Are you busy at lunch, or can I run something for work by you?

The reply came swiftly.

Of course. Let me know when you've seen your last patient this morning.

Thank you, she typed back.

As usual, they bought lunch from Claire's and headed up to the cliffs.

'So what did you want to run by me?' Oliver asked.

'I had an elderly patient this morning—she's diabetic, and she's had a few falls. I'm sending the occupational health team out to her to see if they can tweak a few things and sort out an alarm she can wear round her neck, but I also checked her balance in the surgery, and I've been thinking for a while that maybe we could work with local instructors to set up some balance and light resistance training for our older patients. Say, a six-week course. That way, we're doing some pre-emptive health work instead of waiting for one of them to have a fall and maybe break a hip.'

'That's a good idea. Some of my patients in London went on a course to teach them the basics,' Oliver said, 'and then they could carry on at home.'

'I was thinking chair exercises,' Gemma said. 'A warm-up, some balance work and some resistance training. One of my friends manages the local gym, and she was saying their studio's not used that much during the day—the gym's classes are all just after the morning school run to grab the mums on the way home from school, lunchtime for the office workers, and in the evenings for everyone else. I was thinking, some of those spare spots could be used for a course. Maybe we could join forces with the gym, and between us we could split the cost.'

'And a gym would have light weights and resistance bands available. That's a good idea.' He looked at her. 'If I'm not interfering, would you like me to help you put a proposal together for Caroline, with a cost-benefit analysis?'

'That'd be nice.'

'OK. Are you free this evening?' he asked.

'Sorry. It's Tuesday, so it's my dance aerobics class with Claire.' She paused. 'Though it's actually my friend who manages the gym who instructs the class. I could sound her out after the class and see how practical it'd be.'

'Great idea. Do that, and maybe come over to mine on Thursday evening if you're free. I'll cook,' he offered.

'You'll cook?'

'Don't look so surprised. I've managed to survive my own cooking for the last decade or so,' he said.

'All right. You're on.' It was a combination of business and friendship, she reminded herself, not a date.

'Is there anything you don't eat?'

'I'm not a huge fan of red meat, but other than that I don't have any allergies or major dislikes.'

'Just an addiction to cake,' he teased. 'OK. What time?'

'Seven?' she suggested.

'Seven's fine.'

'How did you get on with the swabs for Mrs Brown?' Oliver asked when he saw Gemma in the staff room, the next day.

'The bacterial one showed just the usual skin flora,' she said, 'but the viral test was positive for HSV1. My poor patient was horrified, even though I explained that it's the Herpes simplex version that causes cold sores, not the sexually transmitted disease,' Gemma said.

'Two-thirds of the population has HSV1,' Oliver said. 'Most of the time it stays dormant, but she might get a flare-up if it's really sunny, or if she's got a cold, or if she's stressed.'

'I've prescribed her a course of antivirals,' Gemma said.

'It's an interesting presentation,' Oliver said. 'You don't often see it on the shins.'

'But imagine how horrible it's been for her—being so itchy in the sticky heat we've had,' Gemma said. 'I've told her to keep up the cold compresses, and I've referred her to Dermatology. How's your morning been?'

'Sprains, strains and hay fever,' he said. 'And an asthma case I want to keep an eye on.'

Gemma had swapped her usual Thursday off for Friday, that week, so she could do the sky-dive; she was too busy for a lunch break, but Oliver texted her in the afternoon to check their dinner meeting was still on.

She played safe and took a bottle of white wine and a hunk of local cheese from the deli. 'I thought you'd prefer this to chocolates,' she said. 'It's a local artisan cheese.'

'Perfect. I love cheese,' Oliver said with a smile. 'You didn't have to bring anything, but I'm glad you did. Come through.'

Even though she knew Oliver was only renting the place for a couple of months, his cottage still felt personal rather than being like temporary home; there were photographs on the mantelpiece and a couple of journals on the coffee table.

'Can I be nosey?' she asked, gesturing to the mantelpiece.

'Sure. They're very obviously my twin and my parents,' he said.

He hadn't been kidding about Rob being his identical twin. The only way she could tell them apart in the photographs was that Rob had shorter hair, in an almost military cut. But, weirdly, it was only the photographs of Oliver that caused her heart to skip a beat.

'So did you train together?' she asked, looking at the two graduation photographs.

'No. He went north-west, so he could take advantage of the climbing locally, and I went to London,' Oliver said.

'He looks nice.'

'He is. He's one of the good guys,' Oliver said. 'Anyway. I assume you walked here, as you haven't asked me for a car permit, so can I get you a glass of wine?'

'That'd be lovely, thank you.' She took a last look at the photographs—and oh, how she envied him the graduation photographs with his parents and his brother. They all

KATE HARDY   121

looked so close, so like the family she longed
for. The family she'd once had.

She followed him into the kitchen, where
he'd set a little bistro table for two.

'Something smells wonderful,' she said. 'Is
there anything I can do to help?'

'Just sit down,' he said with a smile, and
took a casserole dish out of the oven. 'It's an
oven-baked risotto. Chicken, aubergine and
artichoke.'

He'd paired it with a dish of baby plum to-
matoes, a green salad and balsamic dressing.

'This is really delicious,' she said after her
first taste. 'I might have to beg the recipe.'

'It's a foolproof one from the internet. I'll
send you the link,' he said with a smile. 'So
how did you get on at the gym?'

'Pretty well. Melanie said that it'd be nice
to give something back to the community,
and she's got a couple of mornings where we
could have a slot for a class. She's prepared to
do some training to make sure she's teaching
the class properly. She suggested doing it with
a nominal charge for the six-week course, and
then a discounted rate for anyone who wants
to do the follow-up classes.'

'So if the practice paid for the six-week
course, our patients would benefit and so

would the community,' Oliver said. 'I've put together some figures from my old practice, showing how much strength and balance training reduces the risk of falls, so we can see the cost savings between paying for a course of preventative strength and balance training and treating patients after they've fallen.'

'That,' she said, 'is brilliant. It's Caroline's first week back, this week, so I'll leave it until next week before I talk to her about it—but then perhaps we could see her together and talk her through the project?'

'That works for me,' Oliver said. 'So do you go to the gym a lot?'

'Mainly my dance aerobics class. The rest of the time, I'm training for whatever fundraising I'm doing. The skydive is this month; I'm doing a sixty-mile cycle ride along the coast next month. And then I was thinking about doing a swimming thing. I'll do it in the pool at the gym, but if you add all the lengths together it'll be the equivalent of swimming the English Channel.' She smiled. 'Just without all the grease, choppy seas and having to wait a couple of years to book a slot to do it.'

'And it's a lot safer.'

'There is that.' She took a deep breath. 'I

have to admit, I'm a bit scared about tomorrow. I've never jumped from a plane before.'

'You'll be fine,' he said, and his belief in her warmed her all the way through.

CHAPTER SIX

FRIDAY MORNING DAWNED bright and sunny. Gemma, who'd worried about the event being rained off, felt more relaxed; yet, at the same time, adrenalin fizzed through her.

Today she was going to jump from a plane. She was going to jump two miles up from the ground. And, OK, it was a tandem jump and the experienced skydiver would be in control...but it was still a long, long way down.

She showered, then dressed in loose, comfortable clothing and trainers, following the instructions that had come from the skydiving company. Her phone buzzed almost constantly with texts from people wishing her good luck, including one from Oliver. Though there was nothing, she noticed, from her parents. Not that they ever wished her luck when she was doing a fundraising event. Would they ever soften towards her and be close again? she wondered. If she was honest with herself, probably not. But she wouldn't give up on them. She wouldn't stop trying to get through to them. She owed it to Sarah to get their family back together.

Even though her stomach felt twisted with nerves, she made herself eat a bowl of porridge, then headed out to her car.

Except the car didn't look right.

A closer examination told her she had a flat tyre. Oh, no. It would take her ages to fix it. She didn't have time; and it looked as if she was going to miss her slot. If she called a taxi, would she get to the airfield in time? She dragged a hand through her hair. Of all the days to get a flat tyre...

'Is everything OK, Gemma?'

She glanced up to see Oliver in his running gear. 'Flat tyre,' she said. 'And I haven't got time to fix it. I was just about to call a taxi and hope it would get me to the airfield in time for my slot.'

'I'll take you,' he said.

'But—'

'It's my day off,' he cut in gently. 'All I planned to do today was go for a run and clean the house. Both of them can wait. Besides, by the time a taxi gets here, we could be halfway to the airfield.'

She knew that was true. 'Thank you,' she said. 'I really appreciate it.'

'No problem. Come with me.'

It wasn't long until they were at his house. 'Give me thirty seconds to change my shorts for jeans,' he said. 'Luckily I was still warming up when I got to yours, so I'm not disgustingly sweaty and in need of a shower.' The cheeky grin he gave her made her heart feel as if it had done a somersault.

He came downstairs a few moments later, having changed his clothes. 'Let's go,' he said. 'Can you put the airfield's postcode into the satnav?'

'Sure.'

Her nerves must've shown in her voice because he asked gently, 'Are you OK?'

'Yes. Well, no,' she admitted. 'I'm trying not to think about the stats of how many parachutes fail.'

'Very few,' he said. 'According to my twin, fewer than one in three thousand people even sprain an ankle when they jump out of a plane.'

'Does he do a lot of that sort of thing?'

'Yes. He likes the adrenalin rush. You'll be fine. Think of the money you're raising.'

Her palms were sweaty and the back of her neck itched. But she couldn't back out now.

* * *

'I really appreciate you giving me a lift,' Gemma said when they arrived at the airfield.

'No problem.' Ollie paused. 'I've been thinking about you. I might as well wait for you. By the time I get back to Ashermouth, it'll be time to turn round and come to collect you, so I might as well sit in the sun with a mug of tea and watch the planes.'

'I can't ask you to give up your day off like this.'

'You're not,' he said. 'And it's fine. You're the one actually doing the skydive. I'm surprised Claire didn't come with you.'

'She was going to, but the girl who was covering for her called in sick this morning, and Friday's a busy day at the bakery.' Gemma shrugged. 'It's fine. I'm a grown-up.'

Gemma was a brave and capable woman, from what Ollie had seen of her so far; but for a moment vulnerability showed in her eyes. 'Hey. You're Gemma Baxter, village superstar, and you can do this. You can do anything,' he said. Even though he knew physical contact with her wasn't a sensible idea, he was pretty sure she needed a hug, so he wrapped his arms round her and held her close for a few moments. 'Go and sign in and do your safety briefing,' he said.

* * *

Gemma wasn't sure whether the adrenalin bubbling through her was because of what she was about to do or because Oliver had hugged her, or a confused mixture of the two, but she duly went off for the safety briefing, training and fitting of protective equipment.

Oliver was waiting with the supporters of her fellow skydivers, and gave her an encouraging smile. 'Hey. I imagine Claire would've taken a photo of you in your gear, so give us a grin.' He lifted his phone and took a snap. 'Nope. That was more like a grimace. Let's do it again.'

'Say cheese?' she asked wryly.

'No. Say yoga and put both thumbs up.'

'What?' But she did it, and he grinned.

'Perfect. Now go earn that sponsor money. I'll be there to applaud as you land.'

Gemma followed the instructor to board the aircraft. It looked impossibly tiny.

'Let's get you attached to me,' her instructor said. Once he'd put the four clips in place, it felt almost as if she was wearing him like a backpack.

During the fifteen minutes it took to get the plane up to ten thousand feet, the instructor did the equipment check and the final brief.

'Here we go,' he said, and the door opened.

A rush of cold wind filled the plane, and Gemma felt goose-bumps prickle over her skin. She was going to be the fourth and final jumper from their batch, giving her nerves even more time to sizzle.

Finally it was her turn. She sat on the edge of the doorway, ready to go. The fields below looked like a patchwork of gold and green; puffy bits of white clouds billowed here and there.

'One, two, three—go!' the instructor said.

And then they tipped forward. They were head-down, plummeting down to the ground in free-fall.

Even though Gemma knew they were falling at a hundred and twenty miles an hour, she felt weightless, as if they were floating on air. She'd expected it to feel a bit like a roller coaster, with all the swooping; but because there were no twists and turns or sudden changes of direction, it was fine.

The instructor tapped her on the shoulder, and she uncrossed her arms, bringing them up in front of her as she'd been taught down on the ground.

It was incredibly noisy.

And incredibly exhilarating.

And somehow it was peaceful, all at the

same time; in her head, she could hear Tom Petty singing 'Free Fallin''.

The cameraman she'd hired to take a video of the skydive reached out to give her a fist bump, and she grinned.

She was really, really doing this.

She brought her hands in momentarily to make a heart symbol, to remind everyone what she was fundraising for, and yelled, 'Sarah, this is for you!' Even if nobody could hear her on the video, they could at least lip read. Then the instructor opened the parachute. Instead of the jolt she'd expected when the canopy opened, it was a gentle, steady rise.

It took them about five minutes to float all the way down. As she'd been told earlier, she lifted her knees and straightened her legs as she was sitting down. The ground rushed up to meet them; but the landing was smooth, the canopy came down behind them, and the ground crew were there to help them out of the parachute and harness.

All of them gave her a high five. 'Well done! Do you know how much you've raised?'

'Unless anyone's donated since I got on the plane...' She told them the amount, smiling broadly. Everyone had been so generous.

Oliver met her with a broad smile. 'How incredible were you?'

'Thank you.' She grinned. 'Sorry, I'm all over the place right now. I'm still full of adrenalin from the skydive.' Which was only half the reason; Oliver's nearness was definitely making her feel all wobbly.

'You were so brave.'

'My palms were sweating, my heart was thumping and I thought I was going to pass out in the plane. Even though I knew it was safe, it was terrifying. The bit where you sit on the edge of the plane, just before you lean forward and fall out...'

'It sounds horrendous. But you did it.'

'All I did was jump out of a plane, strapped to someone else.'

'You're still amazing,' he countered.

She took off the kit, went to the debriefing, collected the website link for her video so she could share it with everyone who'd supported her, then sent a round-robin text to tell everyone she was down safely and she'd done it.

'So what's the plan now?' he asked.

'Home, please. I need to change that flat tyre.'

'Tell you what. Make me a cheese toastie, and I'll fix it for you.'

'But you've already rescued me once today.

It feels as if I'm taking advantage of you.'
Taking advantage of him. That could have
another meaning. And the vision of Oliver
all rumpled and lazy—smiling, after making
love with her—made the blood rush straight
to her face.

'You're not taking advantage of me,' he
said.

Was it her imagination or was there extra
colour in his cheeks, too? Was he remem-
bering that kiss on the beach and wondering
what it would be like if it happened again?
For a moment, she couldn't breathe.

'If anything,' he said, 'you're doing me a
favour because I can put off doing the chores.'

'Maybe I can do some chores for you in
exchange, then,' she said.

'Five ironed shirts for a flat tyre?'

'Bargain,' she said. 'Let's collect your ironing on the way back.'

'Deal,' he said.

By the time he'd finished changing her
tyre, she'd ironed five shirts and had the
toasted cheese sandwiches ready to go.

'Thank you for saving me from the tyranny
of the ironing board,' he said.

'Thank *you* for putting the spare tyre on
for me,' she said. 'I'll call in to the tyre place
this afternoon and get it sorted out.'

'You're very welcome.'

Once he'd eaten his sandwich, he smiled at her. 'I'll let you get on with the rest of your day. See you at The Anchor tonight for the skydive celebrations.'

'Thanks, Oliver. For everything.'

And his smile made her feel as if the world was full of sunshine.

That evening, when Gemma went to The Anchor to meet up with her friends and colleagues, people seemed to be congratulating her from the moment she walked through the door. She was greeted with hugs, offers of extra sponsorship, and glasses of Prosecco mixed with raspberry liqueur.

The landlord took the website address and password from Gemma and showed the skydive on the pub's large television screen, and everyone cheered at the moment when she jumped out of the plane.

Although the room was busy, she was very aware that Oliver was with the rest of the practice team.

'Hey. You were incredible,' he said.

Did he really think that? The idea made her feel all warm and glowing.

And why had she not noticed before just

how blue his eyes were, and how beautiful his mouth was?

'All I did was jump out of a plane. And people have been so generous. If the money helps with the research and it stops another family having to lose their Sarah...' Her throat felt tight.

As if he guessed what was going through her head, he wrapped his arms round her. 'You're making a difference.'

And now her knees really had turned to jelly.

Being held by Oliver Langley made her all in a spin. She was so aware of him: the warmth of his body, his strength, the citrus scent of his shower gel. She almost—almost—closed her eyes and tipped her head back, inviting a kiss. It was scary how much she wanted him to kiss her.

But then the noise of their surroundings rushed in at her.

They were in the village pub. In front of everyone. And she was in danger of acting very inappropriately.

She took one tiny step back; he released her, but she noticed that he was looking at her mouth. So did he feel this weird pull of attraction, too? She wasn't quite sure how to broach it. Not here, not now; but maybe the next time they spent time together—as friends—she'd be brave and suggest doing something together. A proper date.

Gemma enjoyed the rest of the evening; when she left to go home, as soon as she walked outside she suddenly felt woozy.

'Gemma? Are you all right?' Oliver asked, coming out to join her.

'Just a bit dizzy, that's all.' She winced. 'Probably too much Prosecco. Rookie mistake. People kept refilling my glass, and I didn't even think about it. I don't make a habit of getting drunk.' At that point, she tripped and Oliver caught her.

'Everyone does it at some point,' he said. 'Put your arm round my waist and lean on me. I'll walk you home.'

'Thank you. And sorry for being a burden. I feel like such an idiot.'

'It's fine,' he reassured her.

Just like that moment earlier when he'd hugged her, it felt lovely to have his arm round her. Gemma leaned her head against his shoulder, again noticing that gorgeous citrus scent. 'You're such a sweetie,' she said.

He laughed. 'That's the bubbles talking.'

'No. You were all starchy and grumpy when I first met you. But that's not who you are.

You're warm and lovely. And you smell lovely.'
She squeezed him gently. 'Oli-lovely-ver.'

'Come on, Skydive Girl. Let's get you home.'

He was laughing. With her, not at her. And
he had a really, really lovely laugh, Gemma
thought.

When they got to her flat, he asked for her
keys, unlocked the door and ushered her inside. 'Let me make you a cup of tea. You need
to rehydrate a bit, or you'll feel terrible in the
morning.'

'Oli-lovely-ver,' she said again. 'Thank you.'

'Come and sit down.' He guided her to the
sofa. 'One mug of tea. Milk, no sugar, right?'

'Perfect.' She beamed at him.

Gemma Baxter was a very sweet drunk, Ollie
thought. She'd made him smile, with that
'Oli-lovely-ver' business. He filled the kettle
and switched it on, then hunted in the cup-
boards for mugs and tea. He'd noted earlier
that Gemma was neat and tidy, and things
were stored in sensible and obvious places,
he discovered.

But when he went back into the living room
with two mugs of tea, he realised that she
was fast asleep on the sofa. It was probably
a combination of a reaction to the adrenalin
that had been pumping through her system

all day and the drinks that people had bought her that evening.

He put the mugs down on the coffee table. What now? There was a throw resting on the back of the sofa; he could tuck it over her and leave her on the sofa to sleep off all the Prosecco. Though then she'd probably wake with a sore neck or shoulder as well as a shocking headache.

Or he could carry her to her bed. She'd still have the hangover headache tomorrow, but at least she'd be comfortable.

He lifted her up, and she didn't wake at all. She just curled into him, all warm and soft. And there was a hint of rose and vanilla in her hair that made him want to hold her closer. Not that he'd ever take advantage like that.

He carried her to her room, pushed the duvet aside and laid her down on the bed.

Not wanting to be intrusive, he left her fully clothed, though he did remove her shoes. Then he tucked the duvet round her, and she snuggled against the pillow. He closed the curtains; the noise didn't wake her, so he pulled the door almost closed and went back into her living room.

He could leave her to sleep it off and write her a note; but he didn't really want to leave her on her own. If she was ill in the night and something happened, he'd never forgive himself.

The sofa was way too short for him to lie down on, but he could sort of sprawl on it and wrap the throw round himself. He'd slept on uncomfortable sofas often enough in his student days. OK, so it was years since he'd been a student, but he'd be fine. The most important thing was that Gemma was safe.

He finished his mug of tea, quietly washed up, then settled himself on the sofa with the throw. He dozed fitfully, and checked on Gemma a couple of times during the night; to his relief, she was fine.

The next morning, he washed his face, borrowed Gemma's toothpaste and used his finger as a makeshift brush to stop his mouth feeling quite so revolting, then went into her kitchen to make coffee. He also poured her a large glass of water, and took it through to her.

'Good morning.'

Gemma kept her eyes firmly closed.

Someone was talking to her. But she lived on her own, so that wasn't possible. Was she hallucinating?

A male voice. Not Andy's Northumbrian accent, so she hadn't stayed over at Claire's—

anyway, why would she stay over at Claire's when she only lived a few minutes' walk away?

And she could smell coffee. So she couldn't be at home, because she lived on her own and there was nobody to make coffee for her. Yet this felt like her own bed.

What was going on?

She squinted through one eye.

Someone was standing next to her bed, holding a mug—hence the smell of coffee— and a large glass of water.

Not just someone: Oliver Langley.

Horror swept through her. What was Oliver doing here? She couldn't remember a thing about the end of the evening, yesterday. Oh, no. Had she thrown herself at him? Please don't let her have reverted to the way she'd behaved in that awful year after Sarah died, and made a fool of herself…

Hideously embarrassed and ashamed, she mumbled, 'So sorry.' Her face felt as if it was on fire and she couldn't look at him. Still with her eyes closed, she began, 'I, um, whatever I did or said last night—'

'You fell asleep on your sofa while I was making you a cup of tea,' he cut in. 'I carried you in here, put you in bed, took your shoes off and covered you up. And I slept on your sofa.'

She wasn't sure whether to be relieved, grateful or mortified. He'd clearly stayed to keep an eye on her because she'd been that tipsy last night. How shameful was that? 'Thank you for looking after me.'

'Sit up and drink some water,' he said. 'You'll feel better.'

Still cringing inwardly, she did as he suggested. And he was right; the water helped. 'Thank you.'

'I'm going to make us some toast,' he said. 'I hope you don't mind, but I used some of your toothpaste.'

'Of course I don't mind. Help yourself to anything you need. There are towels in the airing cupboard and a spare toothbrush in the bathroom cabinet.'

'Actually, I used my finger.' He grinned. 'Took me right back to being a student.'

'I'm so sorry,' she said again. 'I don't normally drink more than a glass or two of wine. I don't know what happened last night.'

'People were topping up your glass while you were talking,' he said. 'Plus you were still on a high from the skydive.'

She swallowed hard. 'We...um...didn't...?'

'No. I wouldn't take advantage of anyone like that.'

'Of course you wouldn't. You're one of the good guys.' A hot tide of shame swept through her. 'I'm sorry. I didn't mean to imply you'd...' Oh, help. She was digging herself into a bigger hole here.

'Besides,' he said, a tiny quirk at the corner of his mouth, 'if I had spent the night with you, I rather hope you'd remember it.'

The heat of the shame turned to something else equally hot: a surge of pure desire.

This really wasn't a good idea.

Oliver was in her bedroom. She was in bed. Fully clothed, admittedly, but in bed. And she'd made way too many mistakes of this type before.

'Let's go into the kitchen and have that toast,' she said.

Paracetamol, more water, the mug of coffee and three slices of toast later, Gemma felt human again, and she'd pretty much got her thoughts sorted.

'So let me start again. Thank you for looking after me last night. I apologise if I made a fool of myself. And—' she took a deep breath, cringing inwardly but knowing this had to be done '—I apologise if I threw myself at you.'

'You didn't throw yourself at me,' he said quietly. 'And there's no need to apologise. You were a bit woozy and you fell asleep when I went to make you a mug of tea. I didn't want to leave you on your own. If it had been the other way round, I'm pretty sure you would've looked after me.'

'Of course. That's what friends do.'

'What makes you think you threw yourself at me?'

The question was mild; yet the true answer would shock him, she was sure. She certainly wasn't going to admit that he was absolutely her type and she really liked him. He'd made it clear he only saw her as a friend.

Which meant she'd have to confide in him. Tell him what a mess she'd been.

'It's a bit of a long story. When I was seventeen,' she said, 'I had a bit of a…difficult year.'

The year Gemma's sister had died, Oliver remembered.

'I didn't deal with it very well. I tried lots of ways to escape,' she said. 'I never did drugs or cigarettes, and I've never been a big one for alcohol—but I had sex. Lots of sex. I kind of went through most of the lads in the sixth form and I earned myself a shocking reputation.'

Because she'd been hurting. Because she'd been looking for a way to avoid the pain. Seventeen, and so vulnerable. Ollie's heart went out to her. The boys of her own age wouldn't have thought about why she was throwing herself at them and held back; at that age, the testosterone surge would've taken over and they would've been more than happy to sleep with her. It wouldn't have occurred to any of them that they were taking advantage of someone vulnerable. No wonder this morning Gemma had thought they'd spent the night together: she'd obviously been taken advantage of before.

He reached across the table and took her hand. He squeezed it once, just enough to be sympathetic, but letting her hand go again before the gesture crossed the border into being creepy. 'I'm sorry you had such a rough time.'

She shrugged. 'It was self-inflicted.'

'Didn't your parents…?'

The stricken look on her face stopped him. Clearly, they hadn't. 'I'm sorry,' he said. 'I didn't mean to trample on a sore spot.'

'They were hurting, too. It's pretty difficult to support a teenager who's gone off the rails, and even harder to do that when your heart's broken,' she said softly. 'They just folded in on themselves after Sarah died. I couldn't talk to them about anything. I couldn't tell them how I was feeling, how much I missed my sister, how hard it was to get up in the morning. So I went for the escape route. Or what I thought was one. It was just a mess and I feel bad now because they already had enough to deal with. I just made it worse.'

'What about counselling?' he asked.

'I had counselling in my first year at uni and that really helped me, but when I suggested it to my parents they pretty much blanked me. They're not ones for talking.' She swallowed hard. 'After they moved from Ashermouth Bay, I never lived with them again.'

'You said you stayed with your best friend's family.'

She nodded. 'Claire was worried about me and the way I was behaving. She talked to her mum about it, but even Yvonne couldn't get through to me. Not until results day, when I failed all my exams really badly. Claire dragged me back to her place and made me sit down with her mum. Yvonne said that it was time for plan B, a chance to get my life back into gear. She said she'd been thinking about it and she and Claire's dad had agreed that I could move in with them. I'd resit the second year of my A levels, while Claire would be doing the first year of her catering course at the local college. The deal was, I'd stop the sex.' She shook her head.

'I think the only saving grace of that awful year was that I'd insisted on using condoms, so I didn't get pregnant or catch an STD. But I got called a lot of fairly nasty names. Yvonne said she understood why I was sleeping around, but that behaviour was only hurting me more instead of making things better. She said from that day onward I was going to be one of her girls, part of her family.' She swallowed hard. 'And it was so good to be part of a family again. To feel that I belonged. That I was loved.'

Ollie was seriously unimpressed by Gemma's parents—however tough life was, however miserable it made you, you didn't just give up on your remaining child, the way it sounded as if they had. But he was glad someone had been there to step in and help. 'Claire's mum sounds really special.'

'She is. And what she did for me… I want to pay that forward,' Gemma said earnestly. 'I'd like to offer a troubled teenager a place to stay. A place to get their Plan B sorted. I want to be someone who won't judge because she's been there and knows what it feels like—someone who offers a second chance to get things right, and the support that teenager needs to get through it.'

'I've only known you for a little while, but that's enough for me to know you'd be amazing in a role like that. The authorities will snap you up.'

'You really think so?'

'I really think so.' He reached over to squeeze her hand again. 'Thank you for being so honest with me. I want to reassure you that I'm not going to gossip about you with anyone.'

'Pretty much everyone in the village knows my history. Though thankfully nobody seems to hold it against me nowadays.' She gave him a rueful smile. 'But thank you.'

'It's fine.' Ollie could almost hear his twin's voice in his head. *You like her, so tell her. Take a risk. Be more Rob.* 'Gemma. I like you, and I think you might like me. We're becoming friends, but...' He took a deep breath. *Be more Rob.* 'I want to be more than that.'

'I don't have a good track record,' she warned. 'I've kind of gone the other way from my teens. Claire says I'm so scared of being needy again, I don't let anyone close. So my relationships tend to fizzle out after only a few weeks.'

'I understand that,' he said.

Gemma had trusted him with her past; maybe he should do the same. 'My track record isn't great, either,' he said. 'I was supposed to get married at the beginning of May.'

'When you gave Rob your kidney?'

'A month before the operation. But he wouldn't have been well enough to be at the wedding.'

'Why didn't you just move the wedding?' she asked.

He appreciated the fact she'd thought of the same solution that he had. 'Tabby—my fiancée—called it off. Her dad had ME, so she grew up seeing her mum having to look after him as well as work and look after the kids. And she didn't want that kind of life for herself.'

'But you donated a kidney. Your brother was the one on dialysis, the one who might have problems if his body rejects the new kidney, not you,' Gemma said.

'Her view was what if something happened to me, too?' he said dryly. 'Though when I look back I'm pretty sure it was an excuse.'

'Do you think she fell for someone else and just didn't want to hurt you by telling you?'

He shook his head. 'I think she was having cold feet. She didn't want to marry me because she didn't love me enough. You're right in that Rob's kidney was an excuse. But the real reason—and I know it's real because she told me—is that I wasn't enough for her.' He wrinkled his nose. 'And that's messed with my head a bit.'

'It would mess with anyone's head,' Gemma said. 'I'm sorry you got hurt. But the problem was with her, not you.'

He wasn't so sure. 'With me not being enough, and you not letting anyone close, we might be setting ourselves up for trouble,' he said. 'Maybe we can just see how things go.'

'I'd like that,' she said.

For the first time since Tabby had broken their engagement, he actually felt positive about the idea of dating someone. Dating *Gemma*.

'I'm going to give you the rest of the day to get over your hangover. And I'm not going to kiss you right now, because neither of us is particularly fragrant.' He held her gaze. 'But, just so you know, I'm planning to kiss you tonight. I'd like to take you out to dinner.'

'Actually,' she said, 'I'd rather like to take *you* out to dinner. And I'll drive. I'll book a table and let you know what time I'll pick you up.'

'That's bossy,' he said, but the fact she was

asserting herself appealed to him. 'OK. But I'll meet you here. The walk will do me good. Let me know what time.'

'You're on,' she said, and her smile made his heart skip a beat. He couldn't remember the last time he'd felt this enthused about an evening out.

Maybe, just maybe, he and Gemma could help each other heal from the unhappiness of their pasts. And maybe they could go forward together. Tonight would be that first step.

CHAPTER SEVEN

ONCE OLIVER HAD LEFT, Gemma showered and washed her hair; being clean again made her feel much more human and sorted out most of her hangover.

And it also gave her time to think about what had happened this morning. Now Oliver knew the very worst of her: but it hadn't made a difference to him.

He liked her.

Really liked her.

He'd told her he was planning to kiss her, tonight, and it made her feel like a teenager again—but in a good way, light-hearted and carefree, rather than in an angsty, world-on-her-shoulders kind of way.

He'd suggested going out to dinner. The place where she really wanted to take him tended to be booked up weeks in advance. But it was always worth a try, so she rang them to ask if they could possibly squeeze in a table for two.

'You're in luck,' the manager told her. 'I've just had a cancellation. I can fit you in at eight.'

'That's perfect,' Gemma said. And it was a very good sign.

She texted Oliver.

Managed to get table for eight. Pick you up at seven thirty? Dress code smart-casual.

Should she add a kiss at the end, or not? Then again, they were officially dating. She took a risk and added a kiss.

He replied immediately.

Seven-thirty's perfect. I'll walk over to your place. x

Excitement bubbled through Gemma's veins. He'd sent her a kiss back by text. And he was going to kiss her properly tonight...

She caught up with the chores, then took some flowers down to the churchyard. 'Hey, Sarah. I've met someone. You'd like him,' she said, arranging the flowers in the vase on her sister's grave. 'His ex was pretty unfair to him and broke his heart. It's early days, but

we're going to see how things go between us.'
She finished arranging the flowers. 'I miss
you, Sarah. I wish you were here so I could
chat to you while I was getting ready tonight.'
But her little sister would always be with her
in her heart. 'Love you,' she said softly, and
headed back home.

Gemma took care with her make-up that eve-
ning, and wore her favourite little black dress.
At seven thirty precisely, her doorbell buzzed.
She pressed the button on the intercom.

'Hi, Gemma. It's Oliver.'

'Right on time,' she said.

'Can I come up?'

'Sure.'

Her heart skipped a beat when she opened
her front door. She'd seen him in a suit for
work, and wearing jeans outside the surgery,
but Oliver Langley dressed up for a night out
was something else. Tonight he wore dark
trousers, highly polished shoes, and a blue
linen shirt that really brought out the colour
of his eyes.

'You scrub up very nicely, Dr Langley,' she
said, feeling the colour slide into her face.

He looked her up and down. 'Thank you.
You look beautiful, Gemma,' he said. 'Your
hair is amazing.'

She'd straightened it so it was smooth and shiny and fell to her shoulders. 'Thank you.'

To her surprise, he handed her a bunch of sunflowers. 'For you.'

'Thank you. They're gorgeous. Was that a lucky guess, or did you know they were my favourites?' she asked.

'You had sunflowers in a vase the first time I came round,' he said.

He was that observant? She was impressed. The men she'd dated in the past had never really noticed that sort of thing. The few dates who had actually bought her flowers had chosen red roses or something pink—a safe choice, and she'd appreciated it because she loved flowers, but these ones felt more special.

'Plus,' he added, 'they make me think of you because you're like sunshine.'

'What a lovely thing to say.' The more so because it felt like a genuine compliment. 'Come in while I put them in water.'

'So where are we going tonight?' he asked, following her into the kitchen.

'The Lighthouse. It's a pub in the next village down the coast—it used to be a lighthouse, hence the name, but after it was decommissioned it was turned into a bar and restaurant.' She smiled at him. 'It's foodie heaven, so I think you'll enjoy it. Plus the views are pretty amazing.'

'Sounds lovely,' he said.

She put the sunflowers in a vase. 'You're OK about me driving you?'

He laughed. 'I might be starchy sometimes, but I'm not sexist. I'm absolutely fine with you driving.'

Gemma was a careful, competent driver. Not that Ollie had expected anything less. She drove them to the next village and parked outside what looked at first like a lighthouse, and then when they walked through the front door he realised that the whole of the wall overlooking the sea was made of glass.

'Does this mean we get to see the sunset while we eat?'

'Sort of. We're on the east coast, so we get more of the sunrise than the sunset,' she said, 'but the sky and the sea will still look very pretty.'

Once they were seated, he asked, 'What do you recommend?'

She glanced up at the chalk board and smiled. 'Crab cakes are on the specials today. Definitely them for a starter,' she said. 'For the mains, just about anything; everything's as local as possible, so the fish is particularly good.' She paused. 'Is it just cake you're not a fan of, or sweet stuff in general?'

'I'm not really a pudding or cake person,' he said. 'Which is another difference between me and my twin. Rob will do almost anything for chocolate.'

'That's a pity, because the salted caramel cheesecake here is amazing. But, since you don't like puddings, I'd recommend the cheese plate,' she said. 'They're all local artisan cheeses, and the team here makes their own oatcakes. Actually, it's really hard to choose between pudding and cheese. I might have to toss a coin.'

He ordered the same starter, main and sides as Gemma. The portions were generous and the food was excellent, but the company was even better. He felt more relaxed with Gemma than he'd felt in years. How weird was that? He hadn't been looking to start dating anyone. And yet here he was, on a first date with a woman he liked very much. A woman he wanted to kiss. A woman who made him feel as if the sun was shining through the middle of a rainstorm.

And now was his chance to get to know her better.

'So when you're not chucking yourself out

of a plane or whatever for fundraising,' he said, 'what do you do for fun?'

'Play with my goddaughter,' she said promptly. 'I have my dance aerobics class on Tuesday nights; if Yvonne is hosting a crafting workshop on an evening or a Saturday afternoon, I go to support her and I'm in charge of making coffee. Sometimes I have a girly night in with my friends; that usually involves cake, watching a film, a glass of wine and a mug of hot chocolate. Oh, and a big bowl of home-made sweet popcorn.' She smiled. 'What about you?'

'I run in the morning before work. In London, I used to run along the Regent's Canal, and here I get to run along the harbour and the beach.' That was something Ollie still found a sheer delight; the sound of the sea really calmed him and pushed any worries away. 'When Rob was in Manchester and I was in London, we used to play virtual chess, though as we live nearer each other right now we can do that in person. None of my close friends in London have children yet, so most weekends I'd go with a group of them to watch the rugby or cricket.'

'I get the running, but cricket?' she teased. 'A game that takes days to play rather than a few minutes. Not my thing at all.'

'Rugby?'

She wrinkled her nose. 'Sorry. I'm not into watching any contact sports. I keep thinking of all the medical complications—the torn rotator cuffs, the sprains, the fractures and the cases of herpes gladiatorum. I'll stick to my dance aerobics.'

He loved the teasing glint in her eyes. 'OK. So we've established that you like sweet and I like savoury; I like cricket and rugby and you don't. How about music?'

'Anything I can sing and dance to,' she said promptly, 'and I reserve the right to sing off key. You?'

'Rock,' he said. 'Rob dabbled with the idea of being a rock star. He thought we could be the next Kaiser Chiefs. We started a band when we were thirteen. He was the singer and lead guitarist, one of our friends was the drummer, and he made me learn the bass guitar and do the harmonies. I can't hold a tune, so I was absolutely pants.' He grinned. 'And so was he.'

'Oh, that's cruel,' she said.

'No, it's honest,' he said, laughing. 'Our drummer was out of time, too. It was fun, but we were awful. Our parents were so relieved when we gave it up. Then Rob discovered a climbing wall and found out that not only did he love climbing, he was really good at it.'

'What about you? Are you a climber?'

'Slogging your way up a sheer rock face, when it's chucking it down with rain and there's only a tiny little rope between you and disaster? Nope. That's really not my idea of fun,' he said. 'I'd much rather sit in the dry, watching rugby. Or playing chess.'

'I don't play chess,' she said. 'But Claire's family is really into board games. We used to have game nights every Friday—anything from board games to charades or cards. We'd have build-your-own fajitas for dinner first, which was Yvonne's way of sneaking extra veg into our diet without us noticing. It was a lot of fun.'

'It sounds it,' he said.

'So where did you learn to do that magic trick, making a coin appear behind that little boy's ear?'

'My rotation in paediatrics. The consultant taught me that a magic trick is the best way to distract a child and get them to relax. There's the coin one, and for the older ones there's the one with the magic envelope.'

'Magic envelope?' Gemma asked. 'Tell me more.'

He ran through the rules. 'You write a number on a piece of paper, and put it in a sealed envelope. Then you ask them the year they were born, the year they started school, how many years it's been since they started school, and how old they'll be at the end of this year. Get them to add the four numbers together and tell you what it is. Then you ask them to open the envelope. They'll discover that it contains the number they just told you which is basically double whatever this year is.'

'That's clever,' she said.

'It's a simple maths tricks but it's handy for distracting an older child when you need to get a blood sample, or you're going to do something that's going to be a bit uncomfortable.'

'I'll remember that one,' she said. 'So today the G in GP stands for "genius".'

He laughed. 'I can't take the credit. It was my consultant who taught me.'

'Ah, but *you've* just taught *me*,' she pointed out.

Once they'd finished their meal; Gemma excused herself to go to the toilet and paid the bill on the way so Oliver wouldn't have the chance to argue.

'Thank you for dinner,' he said as they left

the restaurant. 'Next time we do something together, it's my treat.'

So there was definitely going to be a next time? Maybe this time her relationship wouldn't all be over almost as soon as it had begun; the hope made her feel warm all over. 'That'd be nice,' she said with a smile. 'Shall we go and have a last look at the sky and the sea?'

They walked over to the edge of the cliffs, hand in hand. Such a tiny contact, but so sweet. She could really get used to holding hands with Oliver Langley. And she wanted more. A lot more.

The bright colours of the sunset had faded to a rosy afterglow, and the moon was a tiny sliver of a crescent in the darkening sky. 'There's Jupiter,' Gemma said, pointing out the bright planet, 'and Mars. If you look out to the east in the early morning, you'll see Venus.'

'In London, I never really got to see the sky properly,' he said. 'Out here, it's magical.' He turned her to face him. 'You make me feel magical, too, Gemma,' he said softly. 'And, right now, I really want to kiss you.'

'I want to kiss you, too,' she said.

He dipped his head and brushed his mouth against hers, and her lips tingled at the touch.

'Sweet, sweet Gemma,' he said softly, and kissed her again.

It felt as if fireworks were going off in her head. She'd never experienced anything like this before, and she wasn't sure if it made her feel more amazed or terrified.

When Oliver broke the kiss and pulled away slightly, she held his gaze. His pupils were huge, making his eyes seem almost black in the twilight.

She reached up to touch his mouth, and ran her forefinger along his bottom lip,

He nipped gently at her finger.

Suddenly, Gemma found breathing difficult.

'Gemma,' he said, his voice husky. 'I wasn't expecting this to happen.'

'Me neither,' she whispered. And this was crazy. She knew he was only here temporarily, and he'd probably go back to his life in London once his locum job here had finished and his twin had recovered from the transplant. Was she dating him purely because being a temporary colleague made him safe—she wouldn't be reckless enough to lose her heart to someone who wouldn't stick around? Or would it be like the misery of all those years ago when her parents had moved and left her behind?

'We ought to be heading back,' she said. Even though both of them knew there was no reason why they couldn't stand on the cliffs all evening, just kissing, the unexpected intensity of her feelings scared her.

'Uh-huh,' he said—but he held her hand all the way back to the car. And he kissed her again before she unlocked the door.

Gemma drove them back to Ashermouth Bay and parked outside his cottage.

'Would you like to come in for a cup of coffee?' Ollie asked.

Was he being polite, or did he really want to spend more time with her? Or did he mean something other than coffee? It was hard to judge. She wanted to spend more time with him, yet at the same time she thought it would be a mistake. What was the point of getting closer to him if he wasn't going to stick around?

Should she stay or should she go?

'Gemma? I'm asking you in for coffee,' he said quietly. 'I'm not going to rip your clothes off the second you walk in the front door.'

She felt the colour fizz through her face. 'Like the boyfriends in my past, you mean.'

'I wasn't being snippy. Back then, you were seventeen and hurting and maybe not in the place to make the right choices for you. It's different now. I just wanted to let you know that I appreciate you've been honest with me about your past and I'm not going to make assumptions or pressure you to do anything you're not comfortable with.'

So coffee meant just coffee. It meant spending a bit more time with her. Funny how that made her heart feel as if it had just flipped over and eased the tightness in her chest.

'Then thank you. Coffee would be nice.'

'Good.' He took her hand, lifted it to his mouth, pressed a kiss against her palm and folded her fingers over it.

The gesture was unexpectedly sweet, and melted away the last vestiges of her misgivings.

Inside the house, he connected his phone to a speaker. 'Would you like to choose some music while I make you a cappuccino?'

'Cappuccino? As in a *proper* cappuccino?' she checked.

He nodded.

'So are you telling me you have a proper coffee maker in your kitchen? A bean-to-cup one?'

'With a frothing arm. Yup.' He grinned. 'Busted. I didn't tell you that gadgets are my bad habit. Rob gives me quite a hard time about it.'

She groaned. 'And to think I've been giving you instant coffee, when you make the posh stuff.'

He smiled. 'It's OK. I didn't judge you.'

'Didn't you?' She raised an eyebrow at him.

'Only a little bit.' He gave her a little-boy-lost look. 'So I guess I owe you a kiss for being judgmental, then.'

'Yes,' she said. 'I rather think you do. Because there's nothing wrong with instant coffee.'

'Would you choose instant coffee over a proper cappuccino?' he asked.

'No,' she admitted. 'But bean-to-cup machines are a bit—well, fancy.'

'They're a brilliant invention,' he said, laughing. 'As I'll prove to you.' He closed the curtains, put the table lamp on and switched off the overhead light; then he came back over to her. 'One apology kiss coming right up.'

His mouth was soft and warm and sweet, teasing her lips until she opened her mouth and let him deepen the kiss.

'Hold that thought,' he said, 'and choose some music.' He unlocked his phone and went into the streaming app. 'Pick something you like, then come and supervise, if you like.'

'My expertise is in drinking cappuccinos, not making them,' she said. But she picked a mellow playlist, then followed him into the kitchen.

His movements were deft and sure, and the cappuccino was perfect.

'If you ever get bored with being a doctor, you could make a decent barista,' she teased.

He inclined his head. 'Thank you.'

She enjoyed sitting with him on his sofa, his arm around her while she rested her head on his shoulder, just listening to music. Every so often, Oliver kissed her, and each kiss made her head spin.

'Much as I've enjoyed this evening,' Gemma said, 'I'm not going to overstay my welcome. Thank you for the coffee. I'll wash up before I go.'

'No need. Everything will go in the dishwasher,' he said. 'So what are your plans for the rest of the weekend?'

'Tomorrow morning, I'm training for the sponsored cycle ride—seeing how far I can get in two and a half hours,' she said. 'But I'm free in the afternoon, if you'd like to do something.'

'Maybe we can go for a walk,' he suggested.

'That'd be nice. Round the next bay, there's a ruined castle. It's really pretty on the beach there.'

'Great. What time works for you?' he asked.

'About three?' she suggested.

'I'll pick you up,' he said. He kissed her again, his mouth teasing hers. 'Thank you for this evening. I've really enjoyed it.'

'Me, too,' she said, feeling suddenly shy.

'Sweet dreams. See you tomorrow,' he said, and stole a last kiss.

On Sunday morning, Gemma did a long cycle ride, setting an alarm on her watch so she knew when to turn round at the halfway point. Back home, she was pleased to discover that she'd managed thirty-five miles, which meant she was more than halfway to her goal. If she kept doing the short rides during the week and the longer rides at the weekend, she should be fine for the sixty-mile sponsored ride.

In the afternoon, Oliver picked her up at three and drove her to the next bay. It was a pretty walk by the ruined castle and down the cliff path to the sands.

'This is perfect,' he said. 'A proper sandy beach.'

The beach was quiet; there were a couple of families sitting on picnic blankets with small children painstakingly building sandcastles next to them with the aid of a bucket and spade. There were three or four dogs running along the wet sand further down, retrieving tennis balls to drop at their owners' feet; and some couples walking along the edge of the shore, ankle-deep as the waves swooshed in.

Gemma slipped off her shoes and dropped them in her tote bag. 'There's enough room in my bag for your shoes, too,' she told Oliver. 'Let's go for a paddle. There's nothing nicer than walking on flat, wet sand.'

'Agreed—but I'll carry the bag,' he said, and put his shoes in her bag.

They both rolled their jeans up to the knee, then strolled along the shoreline. The sea was deliciously cool against their skin in the heat of the afternoon.

'This is my idea of the perfect afternoon,' he said.

She smiled at him. 'Mine, too.'

They didn't need to chatter; just walking together, hand in hand, was enough. Oliver felt so familiar that it was as if she'd known him for years, not just a few short weeks. Gemma couldn't remember ever feeling so relaxed with someone she was dating. It took her a while to work out just what it was about Oliver: but then she realised.

She trusted him.

He'd seen her at her worst, and he hadn't rejected her. He hadn't taken advantage of her, either; instead, he'd looked after her. Cherished her. Made her feel special.

But then Gemma glanced out to sea and noticed something. 'Oliver, do you see those two boys swimming a bit further out? They look as if they're in trouble.'

He followed her gaze. 'I agree. Do you get rip tides here?'

'Thankfully, not in this bay,' she said. 'But there aren't any lifeguards on this beach, just the public rescue equipment. Do you mind hanging onto my bag and I'll go and see what I can do?' When she could see him about to protest, she reminded him gently, 'It's not that long since the transplant. If you overexert yourself or get an infection, you'll regret it.'

'I know you have a point,' he said, 'but I feel useless.'

'You won't be useless at all,' she said. 'You can call the ambulance, because it's pretty obvious at least one of them is going to need treatment. Don't worry, I'm not going to do anything stupid and I won't put myself in danger—because that just means another person will need rescuing.'

'You two out there! If you're OK,' she yelled to the boys, 'wave to me!'

One of the boys was clearly struggling to stay afloat, submerging completely from time to time; the other looked panicky, and neither of them waved back at her.

'I'm going in,' she said to Oliver. 'Call the ambulance.'

She ran up to the bright orange housing containing the lifebuoy ring, then went back to the sea. Although she and Oliver been walking at the edge of the sea, with the waves swishing round their ankles, the water felt colder than she'd expected. She swam out to them, knowing that Oliver was calling for back-up medical help. But, in the short time it took her to reach them, the struggling boy had gone under again, and this time he hadn't bobbed back up.

She dived under the waves and managed to find him and get him to the surface.

'I'm not sure whether you can hear me or not,' she said, 'but you're safe. Don't struggle. I'm taking you back to shore.' She trod water for a moment, holding him up, and turned to the other boy. 'I know you're scared and tired, but grab this ring and try to follow me back to shore. Don't worry about being fast. Just keep going and focus on one stroke at a time. I'll come back for you and help you, but I need to get your friend to shore first.'

'My brother,' the other boy said, his voice quavery and full of fear. 'His name's Gary.'

'OK. I've got him and I'll get him back to shore,' she reassured him. 'You're not on your own. Try and get to a place where you can get both feet on the ground and your head's above water, and I'll come back for you.'

She focused on getting Gary back to the shore. Ollie was there to meet her, and a couple of other people had clearly noticed what was going on and had gathered beside him.

'The ambulance is on its way here,' he said.

'Good. This is Gary. His brother's still out there, trying to make his way in,' she said. 'He's got a lifebuoy but I said I'd go back to help him.'

'I'll go,' one of the men said. 'I'm a strong swimmer. Oliver said you were both medics, so you'll be needed more here.'

'Thanks,' she said.

'People are bringing towels and blankets,' Oliver said, and helped her to carry Gary to a towel that someone had spread out.

'Brilliant,' she said gratefully. 'He went under a few times, and I'm not sure whether he's still breathing. I just wanted to get him back here so we could do something.'

Oliver knelt next to the boy and gently shook his shoulder. 'Gary? Can you hear me? Open your eyes for me.'

The boy didn't respond.

He and Gemma exchanged a glance. This wasn't a good sign.

'Checking his airway,' Oliver said, tilting the boy's head back and lifting his chin. 'Clear,' he said. But he frowned as he checked the boy's breathing. 'I can't feel any breath on my cheek, I can't hear breathing sounds, and his chest isn't moving, so I'm going to start CPR. Is the other boy OK?'

Gemma looked over to the sea. 'Looks it. The guy who went in to help him—they're close enough to be walking in, now,' she said.

'Good.' Oliver started giving chest compressions, keeping to the beat of the song 'Stayin' Alive'.

Gemma knew that chest compressions were their best chance of keeping him alive. But she also knew that giving chest compressions meant a lot of exertion, and it really hadn't been that long since Oliver had donated a kidney to his brother.

'Come on, Gary, you're not going to die on me,' Oliver said.

'Let me take over for a couple of minutes,' Gemma said. 'We'll split it between us so neither of us gets too tired.'

The other boy ran over and threw himself

down next to them. 'Is my brother all right? He's not going to die, is he?'

'Not on our watch, I hope,' Oliver said. 'Can you tell us what happened?'

'We were swimming. Not far out, because we're not that stupid. And we haven't been drinking or anything. We just wanted to have a bit of fun. But then Gary went under. He said he was getting cramp in his foot and he couldn't swim any more. I tried to get him but I couldn't.' The boy's face was pale with fear. 'He can't die. He can't. Our parents will never forgive me.'

Gemma knew how that felt. 'We're not going to let him die,' she said, and kept doing the compressions.

The man who'd helped with the rescue came over, carrying the lifebuoy. 'I'll put this back,' he said.

At that point, to Gemma's relief, Gary started to cough. Oliver helped her roll the boy onto his side. As she'd expected, his stomach contents gushed out of his mouth; there seemed to be a huge amount of salty water. But at least he was breathing,

'What's your name?' Oliver asked the older boy.

'Ethan.'

'Ethan, we've got an ambulance on the

way. You might want to find your parents and grab your stuff.'

'There's just me and Gary here. Our parents wanted to go and see some garden or other. We said we wanted to stay here, because gardens are boring. We just wanted to have a sw—' Ethan broke off, almost sobbing.

'It's OK,' Oliver said. 'Gary's going to be OK. Go and find your stuff and come back to us.'

Other people had brought towels and blankets, and between them Gemma and Oliver put Gary into the recovery position and covered him with towels to keep him warm.

By the time Ethan got back with their things, the paramedics had arrived. They took over sorting out Gary's breathing and Ollie helped them get Gary onto a scoop so they could take him back to the ambulance.

'Looks as if you could do with checking over, too, lad,' one of the paramedics said to Ethan. 'Come on. We'll get you sorted out.'

'Can we call your mum and dad for you?' Gemma asked.

'No, I'll call my mum.' Ethan swallowed hard. 'Thank you, everyone. But especially you,' he said to Gemma. 'You saved my brother's life.'

'Next time you swim in the sea, make sure

you warm up your muscles properly before you go in, because then you're less likely to get cramp,' she said, clapping his shoulder. 'Take care.'

'He has a point,' Ollie said when the paramedics had gone. 'Without you bringing Gary in he'd have drowned, and Ethan was struggling as well—if you hadn't given him that lifebuoy, he could've drowned, too.'

She shrugged. 'Anyone else would've done the same as me.'

Why wouldn't she accept a genuine compliment? Why did she do herself down? he wondered. 'Impressive swimming, Nurse Practitioner Baxter.'

'Not really.' She shrugged again. 'Growing up in a seaside town means you do all your swimming safety training actually in the sea, with the coastguard trainers.'

'I did mine in the pool round the corner from school,' he said. 'The whole thing with the pyjamas as a float.'

'A pool's good. But I'm glad I did my training in the sea. Open water's a bit different—if nothing else, it's colder and there's the tide to think about. Are you OK?' she asked.

'Doing CPR didn't overexert me, if that's what you were worrying about. But right now

I think I need to get you home so you can get out of those wet clothes. Sorry, I don't have a towel or spare clothes in the car I can offer you.'

'That's not a problem, but I don't want to ruin your car seat. Do you have a plastic bag I can sit on?' she asked.

'No, but I have a foil blanket.'

She blinked. 'Seriously?'

'Seriously.' When they got back to the car, Ollie fished the foil blanket out of the glove compartment.

'So how come you keep a foil blanket in your car?' she asked.

'It's a mix of my mum and my brother. Because Rob does the mountain rescue stuff, he always has a foil blanket with him. When our parents moved here, he made them keep one in the car in case they ever get stuck somewhere; and then Mum made me put one in my car.'

'It feels a bit of a waste, using it to sit on, but I guess at least it'll keep your seat dry. I'll buy you a replacement,' she said.

Ollie smiled at her. 'It's fine—you look like a mermaid with wet hair.'

'It's going to be impossible by the time I get home.' She plaited it roughly.

'Let's get you home,' he said, and drove them back to her flat.

'You're welcome to come in for a cup of horrible instant coffee, given that I don't have a posh coffee machine like you do,' she said with a smile.

He laughed. 'I might go for tea, in that case, but only if you're sure.'

'I'm sure. Put the kettle on and make yourself whatever you want to drink. Everything's in a logical place. I'll be as quick as I can.'

By the time she'd showered and washed her hair, dressed in dry clothes again and put her wet things in the washing machine, Ollie had made himself a mug of tea and her a mug of coffee.

'Thank you,' she said gratefully. 'I could do with this.'

He raised his mug to her. 'To you. Without you, there could be a family in mourning right now.'

'To us,' she corrected. 'Without you giving him CPR, Gary wouldn't have stood a chance.'

He grimaced. 'It still feels weird, the post-Covid "don't give rescue breaths" protocol.'

'Circulation's the really important thing, though,' Gemma pointed out. 'If your heart stops, you die; if you collapse, you need chest compressions getting your circulation going more than you need breaths inflating your lungs.'

'I know, but it still feels a bit off,' he said.

'I'm going to ring the hospital and see how Gary is,' she said. When she put the phone down, she looked relieved. 'They said he's comfortable—but, then, that's the usual hospital comment to anyone who isn't family—and his parents are with him. I've given them my number if Gary and Ethan's parents want to get in touch.'

'This wasn't quite what I had in mind for a romantic afternoon stroll,' he said ruefully.

'No, but we've made a difference to someone, and that's a good thing,' she said.

He kissed her. 'Yes. It's a very good thing.'

CHAPTER EIGHT

OVER THE NEXT couple of weeks, Gemma and Oliver grew closer. It was fast becoming the happiest summer she could ever remember. On the evenings and weekends when she wasn't at a gym class or helping Yvonne with an event or already had arrangements with friends, she spent her time with Oliver—everything from dinner to walking on the beach, to watching the sunset on the cliffs and watching the stars come out over the sea. No pressure, no regrets or baggage: just enjoying each other's company.

Walking hand in hand in the famous rose garden at Alnwick with Oliver was the most romantic Saturday afternoon Gemma had ever spent. The sun was bright but not fiercely hot; the scent of the flowers was incredibly strong and made her feel as if they were strolling through an enchanted storybook garden. And when Oliver pulled her into a secluded arbour and stole a kiss, it made her feel as if the air around them was sparkling with happiness.

Even the monthly visit to her parents, the next day, was bearable this time.

'I went to the rose garden at Alnwick yesterday,' she said. 'It's really amazing. I've never seen so many roses in one place before.'

'That's nice,' her mum said. The usual shutdown. Except this time it didn't hurt as much. Being with Oliver had taught Gemma to look at things a little differently. He appreciated her for who she was—and maybe she didn't need to change her parents. Maybe it was time for her to face the fact that this was the best she was going to get. So instead of feeling miserable that they wouldn't—or couldn't—respond, she should see not having a fight with them as a win.

'I took some photos to show you,' she said brightly, and opened up the app in her phone. 'I nearly bought you a rose bush in the shop, but then I thought it might be nice to choose one together.'

'We'll see,' her father said.

Meaning no.

'OK. We'll put a date in the diary, have a nice afternoon together—with tea and scones—and then I'll buy you a rose bush. Or another plant, if you don't want to be bothered with roses,' she said.

Even though she didn't manage to pin them down to an actual date, they hadn't rejected her out of hand. This was progress, of sorts.

Better still, she had Oliver to go back to at the end of the day. Instead of feeling lonely and hopeless, the way she usually did after seeing her parents, she'd be spending the evening with someone who *did* want to spend time with her.

'How was your visit?' he asked.

'They actually looked at the photographs of Alnwick,' she said. 'And I got a smile.'

Ollie's heart ached for her. If he'd been in her shoes, he knew his parents would've wanted to spend as much time as they could with him, rather than push him away. 'A smile is good,' he said. But he rather thought she needed a hug, and held her close.

Taking her out for dinner would be the easy option; he wanted to make her feel special and cherished. So he'd do something for her instead of paying someone else to do it. 'How about I make us dinner? We could sit in the garden in the sun, with a glass of wine, and just chill.'

'That would be lovely. Can I help make dinner?'

He was about to say no, he wanted to spoil her, but then he realised: she'd said before that her parents stonewalled her. Right now, she needed to feel included. 'Sure. But I'll fine you a kiss for every time you get under my feet in my little galley kitchen,' he said, keeping it light.

'Challenge accepted. And I'll fine you two kisses for getting under my feet.' Her smile reached her eyes, this time, and he knew he'd said the right thing.

On Monday, they had a meeting with Caroline, the head of the practice, about the strength and balance classes for the elderly.

'It was Gemma's idea,' Oliver said. 'But I have friends whose practices have trialled something like this and they shared their stats with me. The cost-benefit analysis shows it'd be a good investment; the amount spent on the classes will be more than offset by the amount saved by not having to treat so many falls.'

'Plus there's the soft side of things: the effect it'll have on the community. I've spoken to Melanie at the gym,' Gemma said. 'She thinks it's a great idea and she's prepared to do the training to make sure she gets the right balance of exercises—um, I didn't actually intend that pun,' she said, when Oliver pulled a face at her. 'She has morning weekday slots available. She suggested a nominal fee for the first six weeks; and then reduced-price classes for people who wanted to continue.'

'You've really worked it out between you, haven't you?' Caroline asked. 'Much as I'd like to go with my heart rather than my head, we do need to look at it in the context of all our patients, because we have to allocate costs fairly. Let me read what you've put together, and I'll come back to you by Friday.'

On Friday, Caroline agreed to the plan.

Celebratory dinner tonight? Oliver suggested by text.

Gemma had been going to Claire's. She texted her best friend, asking if she could invite Oliver.

So I get to meet him properly? YES!

That was the immediate reply.
She texted Oliver.

I'm at Claire's for dinner. Come with me?

Would he think this was taking things too fast, meeting her best friend so soon?

Fortunately she had work to distract her—including a call with Mrs Brown, whose itchy rash had disappeared before the dermatology department could do a biopsy.

And then Oliver texted her back.

I'd love to. What are C's favourite flowers?

She almost sagged in relief.

You really don't have to take flowers, but gerberas.

Good. Let me know what time.

Meeting Gemma's best friend. That was a sign she was letting him a lot closer, Ollie thought. Which was a good thing.

At the same time, he felt faintly intimidated. He knew that Claire would assess him—just as Rob would assess Gemma, if Ollie let them meet each other. And he was pretty sure that the uppermost question in Claire's mind would be whether he'd be good for Gemma or if he'd hurt her.

He hoped he knew the answer, but all he could do was be himself.

After work, he bought a large bunch of zingy orange gerberas and a bottle of good red wine. He didn't have a clue what kind of gift to take a three-year-old, but Gemma had mentioned reading stories to her goddaughter, so he asked for a recommendation in the village bookshop and came out with a book he hoped Scarlett didn't already have.

From what Gemma had said, they'd arrive at just about bedtime for Scarlett, so she'd get a cuddle and a story.

Claire greeted them both with a hug. 'Nice to meet you properly, Oliver,' she said.

'And you,' he replied. 'Thank you for inviting me.' He handed over the gifts he'd brought.

'That's so sweet of you.' She beamed at him. 'And to think of Scarlett, too? Thank you so much. Come through and I'll get you a drink.'

In the living room, Gemma scooped up her goddaughter, who flung her arms round Gemma's neck, squealing, 'Aunty Gemma!'

'Oliver, this is Andy and Scarlett,' Gemma introduced him quickly. 'This is my friend Oliver.'

Andy nodded and smiled.

'Hello,' Scarlett said shyly.

'Oliver brought you something nice,' Claire said, and gave Scarlett the book.

'It's a story about a mermaid!' Scarlett said with a gasp of delight, looking at the front cover. 'Can we read it now, Aunty Gemma?'

Claire coughed. 'Words missing, Scarlett. What do you say to Oliver?'

'Thank you, Oliver,' the little girl said solemnly.

'My pleasure,' Oliver said.

'Come and read it with us,' Gemma said.

And somehow he found himself doing the voice of the shark, who became best friends with the mermaid.

It gave Ollie a jolt.

Sitting here with Gemma, a little girl cuddled between them, reading a story… It was lovely. Sweet, domesticated, and exactly what he'd hoped for when he'd been engaged to Tabby. He wanted to settle down. Have a family. Read stories, build sandcastles, maybe have a cat or dog.

Except he didn't know what Gemma wanted. Did she want to settle down and have a family? She'd spoken about offering a home for a troubled teen; what about babies?

It was too soon to discuss that. He'd known Gemma for a few weeks, and they'd barely started dating. What did she want from a partner? Would he be enough for her? He'd always thought of himself as grounded and sensible, but since Tabby had told him he wasn't enough for her it had made him doubt himself, wonder if instead he was staid and boring. And Gemma herself had said that her relationships tended to fizzle out. They'd agreed to see how things went between them. He really should stop thinking about the future and concentrate on the here and now.

But Ollie still felt as if he fitted here. Once Scarlett was in bed, asleep, and Claire had served the best lasagne he'd ever eaten, he found it easy to chat to Gemma's best friend and her husband, as if he'd known them for years.

Even when he insisted on helping clear up in the kitchen and Claire grilled him, he still felt comfortable.

'Just be careful with her,' Claire said quietly. 'She's not had a great time, the last few years.'

'You and your family made a difference, though,' he said, equally quietly.

'She told you?' Claire looked surprised.

He nodded. 'About Sarah, about her difficult year and about moving in with your family. I'm glad she had you all looking out for her.'

'I don't want to see her hurt again,' Claire said.

'I won't hurt her,' Ollie promised. 'I know she's special.'

Claire gave him a long, assessing gaze. 'I believe you. The question is, will she?'

It gave Ollie pause for thought, but he still found himself becoming closer to Gemma as the next week ticked past. And closer to Ashermouth Bay, too; in London, neighbours could pass you in the street without having a clue that you lived next door. Here, everyone knew everyone. When he went for his morning run, people would wave or call a greeting across the street. If he popped out to the shops, he'd bump into patients who'd stop for a chat, and not just about their health.

Ollie really liked being part of the community here. Being on the surgery's pub quiz team, joining in with all the jokes and good-natured teasing, being right in the middle of things. He was beginning to think that this was exactly where he belonged. And maybe he should think about staying here instead of going back to London.

* * *

On Tuesday morning, Ollie had a nervous patient. 'How can I help, Mrs Parker?' he asked.

'It's my little boy,' she said. 'Yesterday, nursery said James was a bit grumpy. This morning, he's covered in spots. I think he's got chickenpox.'

'I had heard there was an outbreak,' Oliver said. 'How old is James?'

'Three.'

'Chickenpox is usually pretty mild, at that age,' Oliver said, clearly trying to reassure her. 'Were they red spots, practically coming out as you looked at him?'

'Yes,' Penny said.

'In a day or so, they might start to blister and be itchy. He'll have a bit of a temperature, he might tell you he has a tummy ache, and he might be off his food,' Oliver said. 'Keep him at home until five days after the last spots have crusted over. Give him some paracetamol to bring his temperature down, try not to let him scratch the spots, and use calamine lotion to stop the itching.'

Penny bit her lip. 'It's not just James, though.' She smoothed a hand over her bump. 'It's this little one.'

'Would I be right in guessing that you didn't

have chickenpox when you were young?' Oliver asked.

'When I was in primary school, there was an outbreak and Mum sent me to play with every single kid who had it,' Penny said. 'But I never got it. And the baby's due in a month. And I read…' Her voice sounded choked. 'If I get it, and the baby's early…'

'First of all, don't panic,' Oliver said. 'We can check your booking-in bloods and see if you've got any antibodies for chickenpox. If you have, panic over; if not, then we can give you some antiviral medicine. It might not stop you getting chickenpox, but it'll be much less severe and it will help to protect the baby as well.'

'Thank you.' Penny's smile was less wobbly now. 'I was so worried.'

'Of course you were,' Oliver said. 'But we can do a lot to help. Try not to look on the scary side. And definitely don't search things on the Internet, because that's where people like to outdo each other on the horror stories.'

'It's a bit late for that,' Penny said wryly. 'But thank you.'

When she'd gone, he rang the hospital and got them to run a test on Penny's booking-in bloods, explaining the situation and that he had a very anxious mum waiting for the results.

'You're looking twitchy,' Gemma said later that afternoon in the staff rest room. 'Too much coffee?' she teased.

'No. Waiting for test results. I had a worried mum in this morning; her baby's due in a month and her little one has gone down with chickenpox—which she hasn't had.'

'Penny Parker?' Gemma asked.

'Do you know her?'

'We were at school together. She's an absolute sweetheart,' Gemma said. 'So James has chickenpox? Scarlett is in his nursery class, so no doubt she'll be bringing a letter home to warn parents to look out for spots and a temperature.'

Thankfully, the results came in half an hour later, and Ollie was able to ring Penny and tell her that she was immune and didn't need to worry.

On Wednesday evening, Ollie was playing a board game with Gemma when his doorbell rang.

'Are you expecting visitors?' Gemma asked.

'No,' Ollie said, and frowned. 'I hope next door are OK. Jim was saying his knee was giving him a lot of trouble. I've been trying to persuade him to come in so I can examine him properly and maybe refer him for an X-ray.'

When he opened the door, he was surprised to see his twin on the doorstep. 'Rob! I didn't know you were coming over this evening.'

'I'm bored,' Rob said. 'Bored, bored, bored. And, just in case you didn't get the message, first time round, I'm—'

'Bored,' Ollie finished, smiling. 'Got it. Come in.'

'If Mum wraps any more cotton wool round me, I'm going to start looking like a very out-of-season snowm— Oh. Hello.' Rob looked at Gemma, then at his twin. 'Sorry, Olls. I didn't realise you had company.'

'Rob, this is Gemma. My girlfriend.'

Gemma's eyes widened for a moment; but then she smiled, and it felt as if the world was full of sunshine.

'Gemma, this is my—'

'Older, and infinitely more charming twin brother,' Rob said with a smile. 'Robert Langley—Rob, to my friends. Lovely to meet you, Gemma.' He shook her hand, then glanced at the table. 'So who's winning?'

'Gemma is,' Ollie said. 'Go and make coffee, Rob.'

'I've got a better idea. *You* make the coffee, and I'll take your turn for you on the game,' Rob said.

Which clearly signalled his intention to grill her, Gemma thought. No doubt this was how Oliver had felt at Claire's. Well, all she could do was be herself and hope that Rob would like her.

'Olls showed me your skydive video,' Rob said when Oliver had gone into the kitchen. 'I'm impressed.'

'Coming from someone who does stuff for humanitarian organisations and is on a mountain rescue team, you shouldn't be,' Gemma said. 'What I did was only for a few minutes. You do it all the time.'

'Sadly, I won't be able to do the aid stuff in future, because of the kidney—I'm too much of a risk,' Rob said. 'So do you do a lot of this sort of thing for fundraising?'

'I'm sure Oliver's already told you—my little sister had myocarditis and she didn't get a transplant in time. I've been fundraising for the local hospital ever since I qualified and came back here to work. They're doing research into permanent artificial hearts.'

'Which would be a huge game-changer,'

Rob said. 'Is it too late to sponsor you for your skydive?'

'Yes, but I do a cake stall at the surgery on Fridays.'

'Cake? Excellent. Make Olls buy some for me. He hates cake, but I don't,' Rob said.

She smiled. 'I will. Let me know your favourite sort, and I'll make it for this Friday.'

'Anything with chocolate,' Rob said. 'So what else are you planning?'

'I do two big events a year. The skydive had to be postponed so the next one's a bit close—I'm doing a sixty-mile cycle ride down the coast next month,' she said, 'and then after that I'm considering doing a swimming challenge, though I'm planning to swim in the pool at the gym rather than the actual English Channel.'

'Good idea, because then you don't have to wait a couple of years for a slot and then hope that the weather conditions will work out,' Rob said. 'Given the cliffs I've seen along here, I assume you've done climbing or abseiling?'

She shook her head. 'Not for me. Too scary. I'd rather walk along the top of the cliffs and enjoy the view in safety.'

'Or along the beach and rescue a drowning teenager,' Rob said.

Oliver had told his brother about that? She flapped a dismissive hand. 'Everyone around here does their school lifesaving stuff in the sea. Anyone else would've done the same thing.'

'But you're the one who actually went in to get him,' Rob said softly.

'Oliver wanted to, but I didn't want him overexerting himself. I know technically he's allowed to swim in the sea again, but there's a big difference between casual swimming and towing someone in. Plus we needed someone to get in touch with the emergency services. It was a team effort.'

'Uh-huh.' But Rob's smile held approval. 'Olls says there are all kinds of things here. Kite-surfing—'

'No, no and no. Be more me,' Oliver said, coming back into the room. 'Your consultant would have kittens if he could hear you.'

'I know,' Rob said mildly. 'He's given me the green light to go back to work part time. Mum's panicking. But I'm going to be sensible. I told her about that bargain we made: I'm going to be more Ollie and you're going to be more Rob.'

'Me being the sensible one, and Rob being the—'

'Almost sensible one,' Rob cut in with a grin.

The bickering, Gemma could see, was purely for show; the way Oliver and Rob looked at each other told her how much they loved each other.

She thoroughly enjoyed playing the board game with Oliver and his brother; despite the physical distance between them over the last few years, they were clearly very close and talked to each other a lot. The same kind of relationship she would've had with Sarah, she thought wistfully. Love and acceptance of each other, flaws and all.

'I like her, Olls,' Rob said when Gemma left at the end of the evening. 'A lot. She's the complete opposite of Tabby. And she's perfect for you.'

'It's early days,' Ollie said. 'And I'm only here temporarily.'

'Don't overthink things,' Rob advised. 'You still haven't decided whether you're going back to London or somewhere else. Stick around for a bit. See how it goes.'

Ollie wanted to. But he still couldn't quite shake himself of the fear. Would he be enough for Gemma, the way he hadn't been for Tabby? Or was he setting himself up for heartache again?

* * *

Two days later, Penny rang Gemma. 'Gem, I'm so sorry to do this—Mum's away or I'd call her. I don't know what else to do. It's Gran.'

Gemma knew that Penny's grandmother was staying for a few days while her bathroom was being refitted. 'What's happened?'

'She's got a really high temperature.' Penny dragged in a breath. 'I don't know if it's flu, or something else.'

The spectre of Covid, Gemma thought, which could be deadly in older patients.

'I'm so sorry. I just don't know what to do. I can't leave James, and—'

'I'm on my way,' Gemma said. 'I'm your friend. And friends help each other. See you in a minute.'

She filled Oliver in.

'The pizza's not coming to any harm in the fridge,' Oliver said. 'I'll turn the oven off now. Let's go. We'll take my bag with us. And my car,' he added.

Penny greeted them with relief at her front door.

'Run us through your gran's symptoms,' Oliver said.

'Her temperature's thirty-nine, she's got a headache, she's been coughing and says it's hard to breathe, and she's tired and she doesn't want to eat.' Penny bit her lip.

'There are plenty of viruses that do exactly the same thing, including summer flu,' Oliver said. 'Try not to worry.'

'Has she mentioned any loss of smell or taste?' Gemma asked.

Penny shook her head.

'That's a good thing,' Oliver said. 'Let's go and see her.'

Penny introduced Oliver and Gemma to her grandmother, and Oliver listened to the elderly woman's chest while Gemma checked her pulse. Mrs Bailey was coughing, and admitted that it hurt more when she breathed in.

'Crackles,' Oliver said to Gemma quietly. 'How's her pulse?'

'Fast. I'm thinking pneumonia,' Gemma said.

'I agree,' Oliver said. 'Mrs Bailey, we think you have pneumonia. You need antibiotics, but the surgery isn't open at this time of night so I can't prescribe them. We need to get you to hospital.'

'But how did Gran get pneumonia?' Penny asked, looking distraught.

'Lots of things cause pneumonia. Have you ever had chickenpox, Mrs Bailey?' Oliver asked gently.

'Not that I remember. Anyway, I don't have any spots.'

'Chickenpox doesn't always cover you completely with spots; sometimes there might only be one or two little ones,' Gemma said.

'And James has chickenpox. I'll drive you to hospital, Gran,' Penny said.

'You're eight months pregnant and you're worried sick. I'll drive,' Oliver said. 'I'll call the emergency department to let them know we're coming.'

Penny shook her head. 'I can't ask you to do that—and, if Gran's got chickenpox, what if you get it from her?'

'I won't. My brother and I both had it when we were six,' Oliver said. 'And I remember because it was Christmas and it snowed, and we couldn't go out to make a snowman.'

'If you want to go with Oliver and your gran, Penny,' Gemma said, 'I'll stay here and keep an eye on James.'

Penny's bottom lip wobbled. 'Gem. I don't know how to thank you.'

'Hey. You were there for me when I needed a friend. James will be fine with me,' Gemma said, giving her a hug.

'He's asleep right now,' Penny said.

'If he wakes up, I'll give him a cuddle and

read him a story until he goes back to sleep,' Gemma promised.

'You're one of the best,' Penny said. 'Both of you are.'

'Let's get your gran comfortable in my car,' Oliver said.

At the hospital, Florence Jacobs, the registrar on duty, examined Penny's gran and admitted her to a ward. 'It's a precaution,' she said to Penny. 'Pneumonia can be a bit nasty. I'd rather have your gran here so we can monitor her for a couple of days and make sure the antibiotics are working. You can come back in and see her tomorrow, and bring anything you want to make her a bit more comfortable.'

'But—what about her nightie, and her things?'

'Call Gemma and ask her to pack a bag,' Oliver said. 'I'll bring it back here when I drop you home.'

'I can't ask—'

'You're not asking. I'm offering,' he said gently.

'I've ruined your evening with Gemma.'

'It's fine,' he said with a smile. 'Everyone needs a friend to lean on from time to time. Call Gemma.'

'You're so lovely,' she said.

Oli-lovely-ver. He could hear Gemma's voice in his head, and it made him smile. 'My pleasure.' It was good to feel part of a community. Part of Gemma's community. And Oliver found himself wondering what the chances were of Aadya deciding to take a little more maternity leave so he could stay a bit longer. He liked working in Ashermouth Bay, and he liked being with Gemma. More than liked.

And, even though Ollie still didn't trust his own judgement, after Tabby, Rob liked her.

Maybe he and Gemma could be good for each other.

Maybe she was the one he ought to let close.

And maybe, just maybe, he'd be the one that she finally let close, too...

CHAPTER NINE

THE FOLLOWING SATURDAY AFTERNOON, Yvonne was running a workshop and Gemma was helping out. But Ollie had managed to get tickets to see a band he really liked and had talked Gemma into going with him. They grabbed some burritos before the show, and were in the queue early enough to be at the front.

'Are you sure about this?' she asked. 'What if someone knocks into you?'

He could guess what she was worried about: his scar. 'I'm fine,' he said. 'Really.' He stole a kiss. 'But I appreciate the concern.'

During the show, he stood behind Gemma with his arms wrapped round her. It was good to hold her close. And on an evening like this: it was perfect, with the buzz of the crowd and the sheer joy of being there seeing a band he'd liked for years. Gemma knew some of their hits and sang along with everyone else, and Ollie didn't care that neither of them was singing in tune. This was just great. Especially as she was leaning back against him to be even closer.

'That was fantastic,' she said, as they walked back to his car with their arms wrapped round each other.

'It's been a while since I've been to a show,' he said.

'I guess in London you have a lot more choice,' she said.

'There's a lot of good music here, too,' he said.

When he'd driven her home, she asked him in for coffee.

And he spent so long kissing her in her kitchen that they completely forgot about the kettle.

'Um. Sorry,' he said, when he finally broke the kiss.

'I'm not.' She stroked his face. 'Stay tonight?'

His heart skipped a beat. 'Are you asking…?'

She blushed, making her look even prettier. 'Yes.'

He stole another kiss. 'Then yes. Please.'

'Mind you, I've got to be up early to do the cycling training,' she warned.

'I would offer to do it with you,' he said, 'except I don't have a bike and, even if I borrowed one, I'm not used to cycling long-distance so I'd hold you back.'

'Fair comment,' she said.

'But is there something else I could do to support you?'

'We could do with another race medic,' she said. 'But that's a bit of an ask.'

'The event's important to you,' he said, 'so I'll support you. Sign me up and let me know the details.'

'Really?'

'Really.' He held her gaze. 'And tomorrow maybe I could meet you at the end of your ride and take you for lunch.'

'I'm going to be hideously sweaty,' she said. 'Not fit to go out.'

'In that case, how about I cook you a late Sunday lunch here, with proper crispy roast potatoes?' he suggested.

'That,' she said, 'would be perfect.' She kissed him. Then she took his hand. 'It's been a while since I've done this.'

'Me, too,' he said.

'There's a bit of me that's…well, scared,' she admitted.

He stroked her face. 'I won't hurt you,' he promised. 'We don't have to do anything. I can just sleep with you in my arms, if you want. Or I can go home on my own, if you decide you're not ready for this.'

'Oli-lovely-ver,' she said. 'I trust you. And I—I want to make love with you.'

'Good,' he said.

'Do you—' she blushed even harder '—have any condoms?'

'Yes,' he said.

'Then come to bed with me, Oliver,' she said.

He kissed her, and let her lead him to her bedroom.

Gemma woke in the middle of the night, her head cradled on Oliver's shoulder and her arm wrapped round his waist. Closing her eyes, she listened to his deep, regular breathing.

Oliver had been a generous lover. Even though the first time they'd made love should've been awkward and a bit rubbish, it hadn't been. It had felt like—like coming home, she thought. The first time it had ever felt this good, this right.

Maybe this time she'd made the right choice. Maybe this time she'd found someone worth being close to.

Finally, she drifted off to sleep.

When her alarm shrilled the next morning, she leaned over to the bedside table to switch it off. Oliver nuzzled the back of her neck. 'Good morning.'

She turned back to face him and smiled. 'Good morning.' The morning after the night before, she'd half expected to feel shy with him; but instead she just felt happy. As if everything was in its right place.

'I'll get up and head for home so you can get ready for your training,' he said. 'See you for lunch.'

'I look forward to it,' she said. 'What can I bring?'

'Just yourself.' He kissed her again. 'Enjoy your training. Come over whenever you're ready. I plan to do lunch for two o'clock, but let me know if you need it to be later.'

'It sounds perfect. Thank you.'

Once he was back home, Ollie downed a protein shake, changed into his running gear, and went for a run along the sea.

The sun was shining, the sky was the perfect shimmery blue of summer, and life felt good. He couldn't remember the last time he'd felt this happy; and he knew it was all because of Gemma.

He'd finished setting the bistro table in the garden when his phone pinged.

See you in ten minutes.

She was as good as her word, too, not keeping him waiting; and when he opened the door she greeted him with a kiss and handed him a brown paper bag.

'What's this?'

'Host gift. I did consider flowers,' she said, 'but I don't get gardener vibes from you. So I thought you might like these.'

He looked in the bag to discover locally roasted coffee—beans, rather than ground, in deference to his coffee machine—and locally made chutney. 'Thank you. That's lovely. Lunch will be another twenty minutes, so shall I make us coffee and we can sit in the garden?'

She kissed him again. 'That'd be lovely. And something smells gorgeous.'

Gemma, he thought, appreciated him. She paid attention and she'd noticed what he liked.

So maybe this time he'd got it right. And it filled him with joy.

It was a busy week at the practice; Penny's grandmother recovered from her pneumonia, quite a few more of the children in the village came down with chickenpox, and Ollie found himself treating sprains and strains from tourists who'd overdone sporting activities on holiday as well as gardeners who'd wanted to make the most of the good weather. Every day he felt that he was getting to know the people in the village a little more, and really making a difference at the practice. And every night, he and Gemma made love, and it made him feel as if the barriers he'd put round his heart were melting away.

Until Thursday evening, when Gemma was doing something with Claire and he was catching up with some journals, and his phone rang.

He glanced at the screen and felt a flush of guilt as he saw the name of one of his colleagues at the practice in London. 'Hey, Mandy,' he said. 'Sorry, I've been a bit hopeless about staying in touch.'

'It's fine. We know you've had a lot on your plate, with Rob and the transplant.'

'So what can I do for you? Did you and Tristan fancy coming up for a weekend? You'd love the beaches here. You can walk for miles.'

'It's not that,' she said. She took a deep breath. 'I just thought it might be better if you heard the news from someone you know, rather than come across it on social media and what have you.'

Ollie had pretty much ignored social media since he'd been in Northumbria. 'What news?'

'Tabby. She's, um, engaged.'

Tabby. Engaged. To someone else.

He blew out a breath. 'Right.'

'I'm sorry, Ollie. I know you loved her.'

But she hadn't loved him. At least, not enough to marry him. And it had hurt so much when she'd told him. It had taken him months to get over the misery of knowing that he wasn't what she wanted: that he'd got it so wrong. 'I hope she's found someone who can make her happy,' he said, meaning it.

'Are you OK, Ollie?' Mandy asked.

'I'm fine,' he reassured her, even though he was still processing the news. 'And Rob's doing well. He's got a part-time post in the Emergency Department at the hospital near here, to keep him out of mischief for a while.'

'That's good.'

He managed to keep the conversation going for a bit, and extracted a promise that she and Tristan would try to find a spare weekend to come up and visit.

But when he put the phone down, he had time to think about it. Time to brood.

Tabby was engaged to someone else.

It was a good thing that she'd moved on; but the news brought back all his insecuri-

ties. Engaged. To be engaged again this soon,
Tabby must've started dating the guy within
days of calling off the wedding. Which just
went to prove that he really, really hadn't been
enough for her.

So was he kidding himself that he was
enough for Gemma?

Yes, she'd let Ollie close to her; but was he
setting himself up for another failure?

The more he thought about it, the more he
convinced himself that he was making a huge
mistake. His job here was temporary and his
contract ended in a couple of weeks' time—
as did his sabbatical from his practice in London. He was perfectly fit again after donating
a kidney. Which meant that he really ought to
think about going back to London.

But that wasn't fair to Gemma, either. He
knew how much she loved it here. He couldn't
expect her to leave the place where she'd
grown up and go back to London with him.

So he was going to have to find a way of
letting her down gently.

The question was—how?

Something was wrong, Gemma was sure.

Oliver had suddenly gone distant on her.
Too busy for lunch on Friday, she could accept, because she knew how busy they were

at work. Suggesting that she have a girly night with Claire and little Scarlett on Friday evening was Oliver being nice. But when he was too busy to see her on Saturday, and went to see his family on Sunday—without asking her to join him and meet his parents as well as seeing his brother again—she started to wonder if she was missing something.

Had Oliver changed his mind about being with her?

His contract at the surgery was due to end in a couple of weeks, when Aadya was coming back from maternity leave. What then? Would he go back to London? Move elsewhere?

She had no idea. But the one thing she was pretty sure about was that, whatever Oliver decided to do, he wouldn't ask her to go with him.

She texted him on Sunday evening.

Everything OK?

It took a while for him to text her back, but it was cool and polite and told her nothing.

Yes, thanks.

What now?

She could be pathetic and wait for him to dump her, the way she'd been at seventeen.

Or she could take control. Be the one who ended it.

When Oliver made excuses not to see her on Monday, that decided her.

She texted him.

Can I call in for a quick word on the way back from the gym tomorrow?

He took so long replying that she thought he was going to say no. But finally she got the answer she wanted.

Sure.

No suggestion of dinner or a drink.

OK. She'd take the hint. And no way was she going to let him do the 'it's not you, it's me' line. She'd been there and done that way too often.

She showered and changed at the gym after her class, then cycled over to Oliver's cottage and rang the bell.

When he opened the door, he didn't smile or kiss her, the way he had last week.

It was as if they'd stepped into some parallel universe. One where they'd never made love, never kissed, weren't even friends.

And this really felt like the rejections from her teens. The boys who'd ghosted her or who'd ignored her, once they'd got what they wanted.

Clearly she hadn't learned from her mistakes.

And how stupid she'd been to think that they were getting closer. Obviously for Oliver it had been just sex.

'Would you like some coffee?' he asked.

But she could see from his face that he was being polite.

She wasn't going to let herself be needy enough to accept. 'No, thanks,' she said. 'This won't take long. I've been thinking…we took things a bit too fast.'

His expression was completely inscrutable. He merely inclined his head.

And this was excruciating, making her realise how stupid she'd been.

'I think,' she said carefully, 'we should go back to being just colleagues.' She couldn't quite stretch it to friendship. Not when he was going to be leaving anyway.

'You're right,' he said.

'Good.' Though there was one last little

thing. 'I understand if you've changed your mind about helping at the cycle race.'

He shook his head. 'I promised I'd help. It isn't fair to let you down at the last minute.'

It wasn't fair to let her down, full stop. To let her close and then freeze her out. Then again, she was as much to blame. She'd obviously tried so hard not to freeze him out that she'd been too needy. No wonder he'd backed away. 'As you wish,' she said. 'Though I think we should travel separately.'

'Of course,' he said.

'Right. Well, see you at the surgery,' she said brightly, and wheeled her bicycle round so he wouldn't see even the tiniest trace of hurt in her face.

We should go back to being just colleagues.

Not even friends. Just two people who worked together.

The words echoed in Ollie's head. Although part of him knew he was being unfair—he'd pushed her away ever since he'd heard the news about Tabby's engagement—part of him felt as if she'd stomped on a bruise. He hadn't been enough for Tabby, and he clearly hadn't been enough for Gemma, either, otherwise she would've fought for him. Or maybe it was his fault for messing it up in the first place.

Backing away from her instead of telling her what was going on in his head. No wonder she'd dumped him.

But he was only here for another couple of weeks, so it shouldn't matter. He could keep up the facade until his contract ended.

Though lunch without her felt lonely; and he was really aware now of how echoey the little cottage was. How quiet, without Gemma chattering and laughing and teasing him.

Somehow he got through the weekend.

And then, the following Wednesday, Caroline asked to see him.

Was she going to ask him to leave the practice early, to get rid of any tension in the staff room?

To his shock, it was the opposite. 'Aadya wants to come back part-time,' she said. 'And I think we have enough work to justify another full-time GP. You've fitted into the practice really well.'

If only she knew.

'So I'd like to give you first refusal of the new post,' Caroline said.

The answer was obvious. For Gemma's sake, he'd have to say no.

As if she'd anticipated his refusal, Caroline said, 'I know you'd need to sort things out with your practice in London, and I'd be happy to accommodate that. So don't give me an answer now. Think it over for a week.'

'Thank you. I will,' he said, giving her his best and brightest smile.

Stay at Ashermouth Bay.

If Caroline had asked him this a week or so ago, Ollie knew he would've jumped at the chance.

But that was before he'd learned that Tabby was engaged again. Before he'd realised that he was fooling himself if he thought he'd be enough for anyone. Before he'd pushed Gemma away.

The answer would be no. It couldn't be anything else. But he'd be courteous about it and do what Caroline asked, waiting until next week to give her an answer.

And then he'd leave.

Go back to London.

And pretend he'd never met Gemma Baxter.

CHAPTER TEN

THE DAY BEFORE Gemma was due to do the sponsored cycle ride, Ollie had just bought a pint of milk from the village shop when he bumped into her.

'Oliver,' she said, and gave him a cool nod.

But her face was blotchy and he thought she'd been crying. Even though he knew it was none of his business and he should leave it, he couldn't help asking, 'Are you all right?'

'Fine, thank you.'

Cool, calm—and a complete fib. 'You're not all right,' he said softly. 'What's happened?'

She swallowed hard. 'It's Sarah's birthday. I'm trying to celebrate the day. But…'

'It's hard,' he finished. And, even though he knew he wasn't enough for her, he couldn't just leave her like this, clearly heartbroken and trying to be brave. 'Do you want me to come with you to the churchyard, for company?'

She shook her head. 'I can't go today.'

He frowned. 'Why not?'

'Because... Never mind.'

That didn't sound good. At all. 'In that case, I'm making you coffee. No arguments. It's what any—' he chose his words carefully '—colleague would do for another.'

He shepherded her back to his cottage; she sat at the kitchen table in total silence while he made coffee. This really wasn't like Gemma; she was usually bright and bubbly and chatty.

'So why can't you visit your sister today?' he asked.

'Because our parents are visiting her.'

What? 'Surely they'd want to be with you, too?'

Gemma wouldn't meet his eyes. 'It's difficult. Her birthday, her anniversary—those days seem to bring all the misery of her dying back to them, and they can't handle seeing me as well. It kind of feels as if they still blame me for having the virus in the first place, though I'm probably being paranoid. And then they remember how I went off the rails and made everything worse for them, and...' She shook her head. 'It's just easier to give them space today.'

Oliver went to put his arms round her, but she leaned away. 'Don't. I can't... Not now.'

He wasn't entirely sure whether she was rejecting him or rejecting everyone. Hadn't she said to him that she was hopeless at relationships? And he'd frozen her out because his self-doubts had got in the way.

'Sorry. I'm not good company. I'd rather be on my own right now. Thanks for trying. Sorry to waste your coffee.'

And she left before he could find the right words to stop her.

Oliver thought about it for the rest of the morning.

He might not be able to offer Gemma a future, but he could do something to make her life a bit better. Maybe.

He headed for the bakery to see Claire.

'I'm a bit busy,' she said coolly, and he knew he deserved the brush-off.

'It's about Gemma,' he said. 'It's Sarah's birthday today.'

'Yes. She's coming over tonight for fajitas and board games, to take her mind off it.' Claire frowned. 'Is that why you're here? You want to come, too? But I thought you and Gemma had...'

'Split up? Yes. It's my fault. You can yell

at me some other time, but right now is all about Gemma and her parents.'

Claire rolled her eyes. 'Don't talk to me about *them*. I mean, I'm a mum myself now, so I kind of get how hard it must've been for them when Sarah died, but I hate the way...' She stopped. 'Never mind.'

'You hate the way they just abandoned Gemma after Sarah died. And you don't get why they're not wrapping her in cotton wool because she's the only child they have left,' he guessed.

'She told you?' Claire looked shocked. 'Well, that's a good thing. I'm glad she's talking about it. But you're right. I wish her parents...' She grimaced. 'Mum's tried. I've tried. They're just cocooned in their grief and they can't see what they still have.'

'Maybe they need someone who didn't know Sarah to make them see things differently,' Ollie said. 'Like me.'

Claire frowned. 'Why would you do that?'

'Because I care about Gemma.'

'Even though you broke up with her?'

'Claire, as I said, you can yell at me about this another time,' he said, 'but I really need to know where Gemma's parents live.'

Her eyes widened. 'You're going to tackle them *today*?'

'It's probably too much, on Sarah's birthday. I was thinking tomorrow morning,' he said.

'But you can't. It's the race tomorrow. You promised Gem you'd be a race medic.'

'Exactly.' Oliver enlightened Claire about his plan.

'If this goes wrong,' Claire warned, 'Gemma's going to get hurt.'

'She's already hurt. If her parents refuse to listen to me and continue to stay away, what's changed?'

'I guess.' She sighed. 'I have huge reservations about this, and I really don't think you're going to get anywhere with them. But I suppose at least you're trying, for Gemma's sake.' She gave him the address.

'Thank you,' he said.

For the next part of his plan, Ollie rang Rob. 'I need to call in a favour for tomorrow,' he said.

'What kind of favour?' Rob asked.

'I need you to pretend to be me, and be a medic for a sixty-mile sponsored cycle race.'

Rob sounded puzzled. 'Why aren't you going to be there?'

'There's something that needs fixing,' Ollie said. 'I need to do it tomorrow, but I also need to be a race medic. The only way you can be in two places at the same time—or at least seem to be—is if you have an identical twin. Which is why I need your help.'

'Does Gemma know about this?'

'No.'

'Olls, I can't pretend to be her partner.'

'You don't have to. I'm not her partner any more.'

'What? But she's *lovely*, Olls. Why? What happened?'

'I'm not enough for her, just as I wasn't enough for Tabby.' Though Ollie knew he had to be honest. 'I pushed her away. Yes, I'm an idiot and I regret it, but it's too late.'

'Olls—'

'No, it's OK,' he said. 'This isn't about me. It's about her.'

'So what's this fixing you have to do?' Rob asked.

Ollie explained.

'And you're doing this why, exactly?'

'Because it's something I think I can fix for Gemma.'

'You're in love with her, aren't you?'

'I'm not answering that.'

'You don't have to. I *know*,' Rob said. 'All right. I'll help you. But only on condition you actually talk to her and tell her how you really feel about her.'

'There's no point. I'm not enough for her.'

'Did she actually say that?' Rob asked. 'You said yourself, you pushed her away. Stop being an idiot and talk to her. She can't guess what's in your head.'

'I need your help, Rob.'

'Of course I'm going to help you. I owe you everything,' Rob said softly. 'Without you I'd still be on dialysis, waiting for a kidney that might not come in time. But it's precisely because I owe you that I don't want you to mess this up. Promise me you'll talk to her.'

Ollie sighed. 'All right. I promise.'

CHAPTER ELEVEN

ON THE MORNING of the cycle ride, Gemma felt drained, but she'd be letting people down if she didn't do the race. She drove to the village where the starting point was and got her bike out of the back. She couldn't see Oliver's car anywhere, but when she went to register she saw him by the race marshals' tent.

Except it wasn't Oliver.

Even though Rob had let his hair grow out so they really did look identical, Gemma could tell the difference between them. Seeing him didn't feel the same as when she saw Oliver.

So it seemed as if Oliver had sent his twin to be here in his place.

Which just proved he didn't want to be with her and he was going back to London. Why had he even bothered talking to her and being sympathetic yesterday?

It wasn't Rob's fault, so she wasn't going

to take it out on him. She went over to him and smiled. 'Thank you for the support, Rob,' she said.

His eyes widened. 'But I'm Oliver.'

She just looked at him, and he sighed. 'We're identical. I even did my hair like Olls does, and I'm wearing his clothes, not mine. How did you know?'

'I just do. Thank you for—well, doing what he clearly didn't want to do.'

'Gemma, we need to—'

'No, we don't need to talk,' she cut in softly. 'But I appreciate you turning up. And I have a race to cycle.'

'Good luck,' he said.

Ollie's doubts grew as he drove to the village where Gemma's parents lived.

What if they weren't there?

What if they were, but refused to talk to him?

Well, he'd just have to persuade them to listen.

When he rang the doorbell, her mum answered. 'Sorry, I don't buy things at the door.'

'I'm not selling anything, Mrs Baxter.'

She frowned. 'How do you know my name? I've never seen you before in my life.'

'My name's Oliver Langley. I work with

Gemma,' he said. 'May I come in? Please? All I'm asking is for ten minutes of your time.'

'Ten minutes?' She looked confused.

'For Sarah's sake,' he said softly.

She flinched, but then she nodded. 'Come in.'

She didn't offer him a drink, but she did at least invite him to sit down.

'Firstly,' he said, 'I'd like to say how sorry I am about Sarah. I didn't know her—but my brother had a burst appendix and severe blood poisoning earlier this year, which wiped out his kidneys. So I know how it feels to worry about my brother being on dialysis, and whether my kidney would be suitable for him. Whether it might go wrong and we'd lose him.'

'Twelve years.' A tear trickled down Mrs Baxter's cheek. 'Twelve birthdays we haven't spent with our little girl.'

'And that's hard,' Ollie said. 'I know how desperately I would've missed Rob.' And now was his chance to tell them. 'I'm a doctor. I work with Gemma at Ashermouth Bay surgery. I know how much she misses her sister. How much she misses *you*.'

Neither of Gemma's parents responded.

'I know it's difficult,' he said gently. 'Every time you look at Gemma, you see Sarah in her. Of course you do. They're sisters. If we'd lost Rob, my parents would've found it really hard seeing me, because Rob's my identical twin.'

That made her parents look at him.

'I would've found it hard to see them, too, because I'd see him in their smiles and little mannerisms. But,' he said, 'it would've been a lot harder *not* to see them. Cutting myself off from them might've worked in the short term, but in the long term we'd all have missed out on so much.' He paused. 'You're missing out on Gemma.'

'I don't think there's anything more to say, Dr Langley,' Mr Baxter said.

'You said you'd give me ten minutes,' Oliver reminded them.

'Gemma doesn't need us,' Mrs Baxter said.

'Oh, but she does,' he said. 'She might look as if she's moved on with her life and she's completely together, but she's not. She went off the rails, the year Sarah died.'

Both her parents flinched.

'I'm not judging you,' he said. 'We nearly lost Rob, and I know how bad that felt. How much worse it must have been to lose your thirteen-year-old daughter—way, way too young. But Gemma still needs you. Both of you. She's a qualified nurse practitioner and she looks as if she's totally together and getting on with her life. But she's not. She spends nearly all her spare time raising money for the local cardiac ward, the one that treated Sarah. She pushes herself outside her comfort zone, trying to help so another family won't have to go through what you all went through. And she's amazing. She did a skydive last month. Next month, she's going to start swimming the equivalent of the English Channel.

'Right now, she's doing a sixty-mile cycle ride.' He paused. 'And you know what would make the difference to her? If you were there to meet her at the end of the race.'

'We can't,' Gemma's mother said. 'It's too late. We don't...' She shook her head.

'She's never going to give up on you,' he said. 'I know she comes to see you once a month and she'll keep doing that. Even though you reject her over and over and over again, she'll still keep trying. You lost Sarah, but you still have one daughter left. She's not giving up on you. Don't give up on her.'

'She was—difficult, after Sarah died. We couldn't cope with her behaviour,' Mrs Baxter said.

'She told me. But she's past that, now. She's a daughter you can be proud of,' Oliver said. 'She works so hard. And she's amazing.'

'Why are you here?' Mr Baxter asked.

'Because I care about Gemma. I can't bring Sarah back, but I can at least try to help Gemma mend the rift with you.'

'Does she know you're here?' Mrs Baxter asked.

'No,' Oliver said. 'I'm actually supposed to be supporting the race, being one of the medics.'

'Then why are you here?' Mrs Baxter asked.

'Because I wanted to talk to you. My twin brother agreed to pretend to be me,' Oliver said. 'So I haven't totally let her down. She's still got a race medic. Though I am going to have to apologise later for not telling her the entire truth.'

'What do you want from us?' Mr Baxter asked.

Had he really not been clear enough? 'I want,' Oliver said, 'you to see Gemma as she really is. I want you to be there when she cycles past the finish line. I want her to see you clapping.'

'You want us to go there for the end of the race,' Mrs Baxter said.

'I know it won't be easy for you,' he said. 'That it'll take time to mend things properly. But, if you take this first step, she'll come to meet you with open arms. And I'm happy to drive you there myself.'

'I don't know if we can. It's too hard,' Mr Baxter said.

Oliver wanted to bang their heads together and yell at them to stop being so selfish, but he knew it would be pointless. And now he really understood why Gemma had spent that year desperately searching for love—and why she hadn't let people close since, not wanting to be let down again.

And he was just as bad, he realised with a flush of guilt. He'd hurt her as much as her parents had, doing exactly the same thing: pushing her away.

'OK. Thank you for your time,' he said. 'If you change your mind, I think she'll be over the line at about two o'clock.' He took a notepad from his jacket pocket and scribbled down the address. 'This is where the finish line is. This is my phone number, if you want to talk to me. And this—if you want to go on the internet and see her jumping out of a plane for Sarah.

'Your brave, brilliant daughter. The one who's still here and needs her family. The whole village is proud of her—but that's not enough. She needs *you*.' He checked his phone and copied down the link to the video of her skydive, then handed over the paper to Mrs Baxter. 'I'll see myself out,' he said quietly.

He didn't think they'd turn up today. But maybe, just maybe, they'd think about what he'd said. And maybe they'd thaw towards Gemma in the future.

He could only hope.

A mile before the end of the race, Gemma saw the cyclist in front of her wobble precariously, and then almost as if it was in slow motion the bike lurched to the side and the rider hit the ground.

Gemma stopped immediately.

The cyclist was still on the ground.

Another cyclist stopped, too.

'Are you all right?' Gemma asked.

'I can't get up,' the woman said. 'My arm hurts.'

Between them, Gemma and the other cyclist who'd stopped to help lifted the bike off her.

Gemma really wished Oliver was there with her; but he'd sent his brother in his stead, because he didn't even want to be with her today.

She pushed the thought away. Right now,

this wasn't about her; it was about helping this poor woman.

They helped her get to her feet; her left shoulder looked slumped and slightly forward, sending up a red flag for Gemma.

'I'm a nurse practitioner,' Gemma said. 'Can I have a look at your shoulder while we call the race medic?'

'I don't want the race medics. If they come, they won't let me finish and I have to do this.' There were tears in the woman's eyes. 'I lost my husband to leukaemia six months ago. I need to finish this for him. I have loads of sponsorship.'

'OK,' Gemma said. 'But at least let me make you comfortable. You look in pain.'

'It hurts,' the woman admitted, 'but I'm not giving in.'

'Shall I call…?' the other cyclist asked.

'No. Because if I'm right and she's broken her collarbone, we'll walk this last mile and I'll wheel both cycles,' Gemma said.

'I can't ask you to do that,' the woman said.

'You're not asking, I'm offering,' Gemma said, 'because it's important to you to finish and this is the only way it's going to happen. I'm Gemma, by the way.'

'I'm Heather.'

They both looked at the cyclist who'd stopped.

'I'm Paul,' he said.

'Paul, thank you for stopping to help,' Gemma said. 'Can I get you to tell the medics we're on our way, when you've finished the race? But make it clear that Heather's going nowhere in an ambulance until she's gone over the finishing line.'

'Of course I'll tell them. But I'm not leaving you both to walk in on your own—you're too vulnerable. I'll walk behind you with my rear light flashing,' he said, 'to make sure nobody crashes into you. And I'll call the race organisers to tell them what we're doing.'

'That's so kind,' Heather said, tears filming her eyes.

'You're one in a million,' Gemma said. 'Let's have a look at you, Heather.' She gently lowered the neck of Heather's cycling top and examined her clavicle, noting that swelling had already started. 'Is it tender here?'

'Yes,' Heather said through gritted teeth.

'I've got a bandage and some painkillers in my bag,' Gemma said. 'I think you've broken your collarbone. It's going to get more painful—and you definitely need to go to hospital for an X-ray to check how bad the break is and whether you're going to need pins— but for now I can make you a sling to support your arm and give you some painkillers. Are you on any medication, or is there any reason why you can't have paracetamol?'

'No and no,' Heather said.

'Good. Paul, can you let them know we'll need an ambulance? Tell them it's a fractured left clavicle and she'll need an X-ray,' Gemma said.

Paul quickly phoned the race organisers to let them know what was happening, and Gemma took the medicine kit from her bike, gave Heather painkillers and strapped up Heather's arm to stabilise it. 'Now, you need to move that arm as little as possible or you could risk doing serious damage,' she warned. 'The deal is, you walk beside me and I'll wheel our bikes. It's only about another mile. Fifteen to twenty minutes and we'll be there.'

'Thank you both so much,' Heather said.

The three of them started to walk along the road, with other cyclists sailing past them.

'So why are you doing the cycle ride, Gemma?' Heather asked.

'For my little sister. She needed a heart transplant but a suitable heart couldn't be found in time,' Gemma said.

'That's hard,' Heather said. 'Was she very young?'

'Thirteen, and I was seventeen,' Gemma said. 'I'm nearly thirty now; but I still miss her.' She swallowed hard. 'It was her birthday yesterday.'

'She'll know. Just as Mike knows I'm doing this. I'm such a klutz. Trust me to fall off and break my collarbone. If anyone had said I would be able to even stay upright on a bike, let alone ride one for sixty miles…' Heather gave a rueful smile. 'Mike was the one for sport, not me.' She swallowed hard. 'I turned him down so many times when he asked me out. I didn't think it could work between us because we're so different.'

Like Gemma and Oliver.

'But I'm glad I gave in,' Heather continued. 'Because those three years we had together were the best of my life. Even the bad bits, when we got the diagnosis and when he had chemo—at least we had each other. And I know he's up there right now, looking down, proud of me doing this.' She looked at Gemma. 'What about your partner? Is he here?'

'No. He was meant to be the race medic, but his brother's doing it instead.' She shrugged. 'It wouldn't have worked out between us anyway. He's going back to London.'

'You sound like me,' Heather said. 'Don't make the same mistakes I did. I'm glad of the time Mike and I had together—but it could've been so much more if I hadn't been so stubborn. We might've had time to have kids.'

'I have no idea if Oliver wants kids,' Gemma admitted. And she found herself telling Heather the whole story, how she'd accidentally fallen in love with her new colleague but she was pretty sure he was going to leave her and go back to London. She wasn't good at letting people close; she was so terrified she was going to be needy and clingy and stupid again, like she'd been after her little sister's death, that she went too far the other way and backed off when they were getting too close. 'And then he went distant on me, too—and it just escalated. I didn't want to be the one who was left behind, so I suggested being just colleagues. And he didn't try to argue me out of it.'

'Do you know for definite he's going back to London?'

'What is there to make him stay here?'

'You?' Heather suggested. 'Talk to him. Be honest about how you really feel.'

'He's not even here today,' Gemma said. 'He sent his brother.'

'But he didn't have to send anyone at all,' Heather pointed out. 'Maybe he thought you didn't want him there—but he hasn't let you down, has he? He sent someone else to take his place.'

'I guess.'

'What have you got to lose? If you let him go without telling him how you feel, he might be being just as stubborn as you and you're both missing out.'

'And if he doesn't want me?'

'Then at least you'll know the truth. You won't spend your time full of regrets and wondering if things would've been different if you'd been brave enough to talk to him.'

Ollie brooded all the way to village where the race was due to finish. He was pretty sure Gemma's parents wouldn't turn up; he just hoped he hadn't made things worse for her. Maybe Claire and Rob had been right and he shouldn't have interfered.

He went over to the marshals' tent to see his brother.

'How's it going?' he asked.

'Fine—I've treated two cases of dehydration, one of saddle sores and one poor guy who skidded across some tarmac and made a bit of a mess of his arm. Apparently we've got someone coming in shortly with a broken collarbone.' Rob looked at him. 'How did it go?'

'Awful.' Ollie grimaced. 'Have you seen Gemma?'

'Yes, and you're in trouble. She knew I wasn't you before I even opened my mouth.'

'What did she say?'

'She didn't give me a chance to explain. She said she had a race to ride.'

'I'll face the music later,' Ollie said. 'Thanks for helping. I'll take over from you now.'

'I'm fine. Actually, I'm enjoying having something to do. Go and wait for Gemma by the finish line. And make sure you've got a seriously, seriously good apology ready, because you're going to need it,' Rob warned.

Oliver made his way through to the finish line, knowing he'd messed things up. He felt as if the world was sitting on his shoulders. He had no idea where to start fixing this.

Why hadn't he just left things alone?

And then his phone rang.

It was a number he didn't recognise. He thought about ignoring it; but right now he had nothing better to do and it would waste some time while he waited.

'Dr Langley?' a voice he didn't recognise said on the other end.

'Yes?'

'It's Stephanie Baxter. Um, we thought about

what you said. We've been talking. We…um…wondered if we could wait with you.'

Hope bloomed in his heart. Gemma's parents were coming to watch her finish the race? 'Of course you can.' He told her exactly where he was. 'See you soon. And thank you.'

'No. Thank *you*,' she said. 'Because you've just given us a second chance with our daughter.'

Ollie really, really hoped she was right.

People were lining the streets of the village where the race ended, cheering and clapping.

Gemma forced herself to smile, even though she felt like crying. Everything had gone so wrong with Oliver. Was Heather right? Should she be brave and tell him how she felt? But what if he still went back to London without her? She didn't want to face rejection yet again.

She plodded on, one foot in front of the other, and kept Heather going with words of encouragement that weirdly kept her going, too.

'I think,' Paul said, 'Heather needs to ride over that finish line.'

'She can't ride with a broken clavicle,' Gemma said.

'She won't be holding the handlebars,' Paul

said. 'If I lift her onto the bike, we can be either side of her to keep the bike stable and we'll steady it while she pedals for the last ten metres.'

So Heather would get to fulfil her dream. 'You're on,' Gemma said.

Between them, they got Heather onto the bike. They co-opted a couple of people lining the route to hold their bikes for them while they helped Heather, who was smiling and crying at the same time as they supported her over the finish line.

The medics were there, waiting to help Heather to the ambulance; for a moment, Gemma thought Oliver was standing there, but her heart didn't have that funny little skip and she realised that it was Rob.

Stupid.

Of course Oliver wouldn't be there.

'Well done,' Rob said, clapping her shoulder. 'That was an amazing thing to do.'

'It wasn't my time that mattered,' she said. 'It was Heather finishing that was important.' She couldn't bring herself to ask where Oliver was. 'I'd better collect my bike and finish officially.'

Paul was waiting for her, and they rode over the finish line together, with people cheering and clapping all around them.

She dismounted and hugged him. 'Thank you. What you did…'

'The same as you did,' he said, 'for a complete stranger. Because we're all in this together. And we want to make a difference.'

'Yeah.'

'I'll look after Heather's bike,' Paul said, 'because I think you've got some people wanting to see you.'

Gemma looked up and saw Oliver standing there. But what really shocked her was that her parents were next to him. Her mum and dad had tears running down their faces, and they held out their arms to her.

She couldn't quite process this.

Why were her parents here? She hadn't even told them where the race was, just that she was doing it.

Oliver took her bike. 'Go to them,' he said softly. 'I'll be waiting when you've talked.'

She stared at him—'But…' She couldn't even begin to frame the questions buzzing through her head.

'I interfered,' he said. 'I'll apologise later, but I think you and your parents need to talk. Don't worry about your bike. I'll go and put it in my car. Give me your race number and I'll sort out any paperwork for you.'

'I…'

'Swap you the paperwork for a recovery drink and a recovery bar,' he said, pushing them into her hands. 'I'll feed you properly later, but you need to replenish your glycogen stores.'

'Spoken like a doctor,' she said wryly, and handed over her race number.

'And like the brother of someone who does this sort of thing himself, so I kind of know the drill. Go with your parents,' he said. 'When you're ready, I'll be in the marshals' tent, where I was supposed to be.'

'Mum. Dad.'

'Our girl. Sixty miles you cycled. And you helped that lass who'd fallen off her bike— you didn't just leave it to the medics to sort her out,' her dad said.

'Well—you *are* a medic. Nurse practitioner,' her mum said.

'How…? Why…?' Gemma cleared her throat and tried again. 'I didn't expect to see you here.'

'Your young man came to see us,' her mum explained.

Gemma frowned. Oliver wasn't hers any more.

'He told us about his brother. How he nearly died.' There was a catch in her dad's voice.

'And he said how much you missed our Sarah. How much you missed *us*.'

'We haven't been proper parents to you,' her mum said. 'Not since Sarah died. We just couldn't get past losing her. And then, when it wasn't quite so raw any more, you…'

Gemma looked at them. She could let them off lightly, brush it under the carpet. Or she could be honest: and that might be a better way. Because at least then any relationship they managed to build would be on a solid foundation, with no areas where they were scared to tread. 'I was difficult to handle,' she said. 'I went off the rails. Because I couldn't cope with losing my little sister *and* losing my parents. Sleeping with all those boys— it made me feel loved again, just for a little while.'

Her dad flinched. 'It wouldn't have happened if we'd been there for you.'

'I'm not blaming you—either of you,' Gemma said. 'What happened, happened. I'm acknowledging it and I've moved past it.'

'Yvonne was the one who saved you. She was the mum I should've been to you. And I was grateful to her for stepping in, because I couldn't do it.' Colour flooded Stephanie's cheeks. 'At the same time, I was so jealous of her. You moved in with her and it felt as if you preferred someone else's family to your own. As if I'd lost both my girls.'

'You never lost me, Mum,' Gemma said. 'I needed to live with Claire's family to get through my exams. You weren't in a place where you could help me—and I couldn't deal with all that extra travelling to get to school. Things were hard enough. And I never gave up on you. I come and see you every month— even though you never come to see me, and getting either of you to talk to me is like pulling teeth. But I promised Sarah I'd never give up, and I've always hoped that one day I'd get some of my family back.'

'He's right about you, your young man,' her dad said. 'He said you'd never give up on us. And you're a daughter we can be proud of. All that money you raise for charity.'

'For the ward where Sarah died. Where they're doing research into permanent artificial hearts,' Gemma said. 'So maybe one day soon no other family will have to wait for a donor heart and risk losing their Sarah.'

'He showed us your video. You, jumping out of a plane,' her mum said. 'And he told us where we could find you today. We watched you help that woman. And we're—' her voice cracked '—we're so proud of you. Can you ever forgive us?'

Gemma had no words. She just opened her arms.

And, for the first time in too many years, her parents wrapped her in a hug. A real, proper hug. The hug she'd been so desperate to have.

'We love you so much, Gemma,' her dad said.

'It probably doesn't feel like it,' her mum said. 'But we do. And we're so sorry we let you down.'

'It's hard for us, going back to Ashermouth. But if that's where you want to be, then we'll come there to see you,' her dad said. 'Your young man's right—it's time we remembered we had another daughter. We want you in our lives. Properly. The way it should've been all along. It's been so…' His mouth moved but no words came out.

She wasn't going to push them into talking more. Not right now. 'I know,' she said softly. 'I want that, too. And I know it's not going to be magically fixed overnight. We've got a lot of talking to do. But, now we've started, it'll get easier. And if we work at it, we'll make it. Together.'

'We do love you, Gem,' her mum said.

Words she'd wanted to hear for far too long. And both her parents had said it now. 'I love you, too,' she said shakily.

'You'd better go and see your young man,' her dad said. 'But we'll call you tomorrow.'

'And we're so proud of you.' Gemma's mum hugged her again.

'I'll talk to you tomorrow,' Gemma said. Tears blurred her vision as she made her way to the marshals' tent. Oliver had seen the chasm between her and her parents, and he'd laid a huge foundation plank across it.

Your young man.

Did she dare to hope that what he'd done— taught her parents to see her for who she was—meant he really cared about her? Was this his way of saying that maybe they had a future together? Or was this a goodbye present, a way of telling her that he couldn't be there for her but he hoped her parents would be?

Heather had advised her to talk to him. Tell him how she really felt.

And there was only one way to find out the answers to her questions…

Ollie sorted out the race admin for Gemma, then went back to the marshals' tent to help Rob. Various cyclists had come to the medics for help as they'd finished, with sprains, strains and saddle sores.

To his relief, his twin didn't ask him any awkward questions, just let him help treat their patients.

Finally Rob nudged him. 'I'll finish up here. You have a visitor.'

Ollie looked up; when he saw Gemma standing by the table, his heart skipped a beat.

'Hi,' she said.

He couldn't tell if everything was all right or not, but he wanted to let her set the pace. 'Hi.'

'Is Heather all right?' she asked Rob.

'The ambulance took her to hospital. Paul's looking after her bike and he's going to take it back to his place for now, then drop it over to hers,' Rob said. 'Obviously I didn't have your number, but I've taken theirs and texted them to Olls so you can get in touch with them.'

'Thank you,' she said. She looked at Ollie. 'Can we go somewhere quiet and talk?'

'Sure.' Ollie nodded to his twin, then followed Gemma out of the tent. They headed towards the sea, and found a quiet spot away from the crowds.

'That was a really kind thing you did, helping Heather over the finish line like that.'

'It wasn't just me. Paul helped, too. She had a broken clavicle. No way could she have wheeled that bike herself without jolting her arm.' Gemma shrugged.

'You could've waited with her until the marshals came.'

'No, I couldn't. It was important to Heather to finish the race and they would've stopped her. She was doing it in memory of her husband, who died from leukaemia, and we were so close to the end. It's just what anyone else would've done in an event like this when they saw someone was struggling.'

Ollie wasn't quite so sure, but Gemma clearly didn't believe she was special. 'I sorted out the race admin stuff for you,' he said.

'Thank you.' She took a deep breath. 'I didn't expect to see you today. When I saw Rob and realised you'd sent him in your place, I assumed...' Her voice tailed off.

'The worst? That I'd abandoned you?' The way her parents had when she was seventeen, and the way they'd stonewalled her over the last few years?

'Yes,' she admitted.

'I saw how upset you were yesterday and I wanted to do something about it. I know I was interfering. But I didn't want to let you down with this, either—which is why I talked Rob into taking my place,' Ollie explained.

'How did you even find my parents?'

'I asked— Never mind,' he said, not wanting to make things awkward between Gemma and her best friend. 'And I was warned not to interfere.'

'But you went to see them anyway.' Her eyes were red, as if she'd been crying.

He'd been so hopeful when her parents had called him and asked to stand with him at the end—so sure that he'd helped them start to reconnect with Gemma. Maybe he'd got it wrong. Maybe this had been the last straw, and instead they'd told Gemma never to see them again. Guilt flooded through him. 'I'm sorry if I've made things worse.'

'No, you made them...' She swallowed hard. 'Today was the first time in more than a decade that my parents told me they loved me.'

Ollie didn't know what to say. It was a good thing; yet, at the same time, his heart broke a little for her. She'd tried so hard for all those years, had refused to give up: yet all that time she'd been hurting. Lonely. Wanting to be loved.

'They told me they were proud of me.'

'Good. And so they should be,' he said. 'You're an amazing woman.'

'But not,' she said, 'amazing enough for you.'

'Oh, you are,' he said.

'Then I don't get why you backed away from me. I don't understand you, Oliver. Not at all.'

Because he'd panicked. 'I just wanted to help.'

'You did. You've built a massive bridge between me and my parents—it's early days and there's still a lot to work through, but we're finally starting to see things the same way.' She looked at him. 'What I don't understand is why you did that. You and I…we agreed just to be colleagues.'

'Yes.' He knew he should tell her that wasn't what he wanted—but what if she rejected him?

When he didn't explain further, Gemma said, 'Heather told me she thought her husband was her complete opposite and it'd never work out between them. She held out for a long time before she agreed to date him—and then he was diagnosed with leukaemia. He died last year. And she said she'll always regret she wasn't brave enough to let them have more time together.'

His heart skipped a beat. Was Gemma saying that was how she saw their situation, too? Was this her way of telling him she wanted to try to make a go of things?

'She said it's important to be honest, to tell someone how you feel about them and not waste time.' Gemma took a deep breath. 'It scares me to death, saying this—but at the same time I know I'll always regret it if I don't. So I'm going to say it. I know you want to go back to London, and I'm not going to trap you or ask you to stay; but I also don't want you to go without knowing the truth. That I love you.'

She loved him.

The words echoed through his head.

She loved him.

But then his insecurities snapped back in. 'How can I be enough for you?'

It was the last thing Gemma had expected him to say.

But then she remembered what he'd told her. How his ex had called off the wedding. 'Is this about Tabby? Are you still in love with her?'

'It's sort of about her,' Oliver said. 'But, no, I'm not still in love with her. One of my old colleagues told me that Tabby had got engaged again. And it made me think. I wasn't enough to make her love me, so why should I think I'd be enough for someone else?'

'Oliver Langley, do you really have no idea how amazing you are?' she asked. 'Look at the way you work with us in the practice. You fitted right in. You're part of the team. You've helped me make some innovations that will make our older patients' lives better. And you've just managed to do something that my best friend's family has tried and failed for do for over a decade—you talked to my parents, you got them to listen to you, and you changed their view of me. You've done what I thought was impossible: you've actually got us talking and starting to heal that rift.

'And, apart from all that, I love you. You make me feel like a teenager again—not full of angst and worry, but seeing all the possibilities in life.' She bit her lip. 'I thought you might have feelings for me, too. Until you backed away.'

'I do have feelings for you. I love you,' he said, 'and I know it's the real thing, because I feel different when I'm with you. The world feels a better place, full of sunshine and hope.' He paused. 'But how do I know I'm not fooling myself? How do I know I'll be enough for you?'

'Do you trust me?' she asked.

He was silent for so long that she thought he was going to tell her he didn't. But then he nodded. 'I trust you.'

'Then believe me. I think you're enough for me. You're the first man I've let close in years and years. You're everything I want in a partner. You're kind, you're funny, you notice the little details, and you make my heart feel as if it's doing cartwheels when you smile at me.' She took a deep breath. 'I know you're meant to be leaving in a few days, but—'

'Actually,' he cut in, 'I don't have to leave. Caroline says that Aadya wants to come back part-time, and the practice has expanded enough that she could do with another full-time doctor. She's given me first choice of the post.'

'So you could stay here?'

'Yes.'

'And is that what you want?'

'I want,' he said, 'to be with you. I've learned that I like being part of a small community—*this* community. I like living in a village where I know everyone and everyone knows me. Where people support each other. I want to live and work in a community where people really connect with each other.' He looked at her. 'But most of all I want to live with you. I want to make a family with you—whether we have children of our own, whether we support a teen in trouble, or whether it's a mixture of the two.'

So he'd remembered what she'd said to him about paying it forward.

'I saw you with your goddaughter,' he said, 'cuddling her and reading a story. When we read that story to her together. And it made me realise that was what I wanted. You, and our family.' His blue eyes were full of warmth and love. 'This probably isn't the right time to say this, when you've just done a sixty-mile bike ride.'

'Strictly speaking, that's fifty-nine miles cycling and about a mile's walk,' she pointed out.

'A mile's walk pushing two bikes and supporting someone with a broken collarbone,' he said. 'Which is a lot more effort than cycling. Gemma, when I came to Ashermouth Bay, I was miserable and lonely and in a lot of denial. And then I met you. And I found out how the world really ought to be—full of love and sunshine. You make the day sparkle. And I want to spend the rest of my life with you.' He dropped to one knee. 'I probably ought to wait and do this somewhere really romantic. But I can virtually hear my twin yelling in my ear, "Be more Rob!"—and your friend Heather was right. It's important to be honest, to tell someone how you feel about them and not waste time. So I'm going to take the risk and tell you. I've learned that it's not the showy stuff that matters: it's what's in your heart. And I love you, Gemma Baxter. I really, really love you. Will you marry me and make a family with me?'

Marry him.

Make a family with him.

He was offering her everything she wanted. More than that: he'd actually got her parents to make the first move, to start to heal the rift between them.

She leaned down and kissed him. 'Yes.'

* * * * *

Look out for the next story in the
Twin Doc's Perfect Match duet

Baby Miracle for the ER Doc

If you enjoyed this story, check out these
other great reads from Kate Hardy

Forever Family for the Midwife
Fling with Her Hot-Shot Consultant
Heart Surgeon, Prince...Husband!

All available now!